AWKWA... ...**...INING...**

Pink BITS

JB HELLER

Pink Bits, Awkward Girls Book One

Copyright © 2019 by JB Heller

All rights reserved.

Published by- JB Heller

jb@jbthindie.com

Cover Design by- JeBDesigns

Editing by- Creating INK Services

Proofreading by- Jenn Lockwood Editing

Formatted by – JeBDesigns

No part of this book may be reproduced or transmitted in any form or by any means, electronic or mechanical, including photocopying, recording, or by any information storage and retrieval system without the written permission of the author, except for the use of brief quotations in a book review.

This book is a work of fiction. Names, characters, places and incidents either are products of the author's imagination or are used fictitiously. Any resemblance to actual persons, living or dead, events or locales is entirely coincidental.

AUTHORS NOTE

Please note this series based in Australia, written by an Australian author, in Australian English. As such you may think there are a few spelling errors, however that's just how we spell things down under.

Thank you and enjoy,
Xox
JB

Chapter One

Reagan

DID YOU KNOW THAT SWANS ARE THE ONLY BIRDS with an external penis? It's totally true—and fascinating, if you ask me. I mean, can you imagine a little hummingbird flying around with a penis? Disturbing, right? But a swan—I can get behind that.

This is the latest fact I've submitted into the Pink Bits database. I love my job so much. Spending my days searching out weird, wonderful, and completely random facts is a dream come true. It helps that Pink Bits Hygienics is my dad's company, and he created the position especially for me. Hell, he created the company *because* of me, and his sisters.

"Reagan, are you coming to dinner with your mother and me this evening?"

Shifting my gaze from the computer screen, I eye

Dad's lean build propped against the doorway to my office. "My stepmother, you mean?"

He rolls his eyes. "Well, yes. Unless your biological mother has changed her mind about removing my testicles with her bare hands. Then she'd be welcome to join us as well."

I cringe at the imagery manifesting in my brain. "Thanks for the visual." I mime sticking my finger down my throat, and my dad chuckles. "Anyway, no, I will not be joining you and The Wicked Witch of the West for dinner tonight. I have plans."

"Plans?" he asks, completely ignoring the jab at my stepmother. He strides into my office and drops into the pink loveseat I have situated by the large floor-to-ceiling window, then props his feet up. "What kind of plans? Plans with a—dare I say it—man?" He waggles his eyebrows suggestively as he speaks, making it impossible for me to keep a straight face.

A snort escapes as I try to hold back my laughter. "No, sorry to disappoint, Daddy. I'm going to the movies with Charlotte."

His shoulders drop. "I want grandchildren, Reagan, and you're not being very proactive about it." He huffs, planting his feet on the floor and pushing off. Straightening his suit jacket then tie, he says, "Just go on one date a month. I'm not asking much. Even without grandbabies, I want to see you with someone. You're twenty-seven, and I've never met one of your boyfriends. It's time, honey."

"Pfft, don't hold your breath. Have you met the douchebags in the dating pool these days? Trust me, Daddy, you'd rather I die an old cat lady than bring one of them home."

When he reaches the door, he pauses and looks back over his shoulder, his fingers flexing around the frame. "If anyone can find the needle in the haystack, it'll be you. But you've gotta be out there looking for it, baby."

Once he's gone, I drop my head into my hands. He's right. But I'm just too awkward for the dating scene. I'm fascinated by the fact that swans have penises, peni, peens, whatever. The point is, it's hardly a topic I can bring up on a dinner date. Any potential boyfriend would run out screaming or think I was into some really weird, kinky shit. And I'm not. I swear I'm only into a normal amount of kink.

Tucking my hair behind my ears, I strum my bright pink fingernails over my keyboard. My eyes drift to the time displayed in the corner of my computer screen: five-fifteen. I'm doused in an ice-cold bucket of self-pity as I acknowledge just how pathetic it is to be sitting in my office at five-fifteen on a Friday afternoon with no intention of leaving until I have to meet Char at seven.

I slump back in my gorgeous rose-print velvet armchair, kick my heels off, and prop my feet on the corner of my desk. This small act of unprofessionalism makes me feel a wee bit less pathetic. But my dad's words roll around my head, refusing to leave me be. *If anyone can find the needle in the haystack, it's you.* I sigh audibly with all the dramatics of a three-year-old beauty queen and flop my head back to stare at the ceiling.

It's not like I don't want to find someone. I'm just not the kind of girl that has man-catching skills. I was never taught, and even if I had been, I doubt I would have been able to master it. I'm not equipped with the required talents. I have no filter, no sense of appropriate conversation, and small talk? Yeah, not my forte.

If only I could find someone as wildly inappropriate as myself.

My phone chirps with an incoming text, and I drop my feet from the desk, swivelling around to riffle through my bag and find my phone. Sliding my finger over the screen, I see a message from Charlotte. A grin tugs at the corner of my lips until the words register.

CHARLOTTE: Babe I'm SOOO sorry but I have to cancel tonight. I'm surfin' the crimson wave and Mother Nature is being an extra cruel bitch this month. I feel like a slasher film is being enacted inside my uterus.

Her description makes me cringe. Char has endometriosis, so she suffers from particularly bad periods—to say the least. It's given her the motivation to come up with extremely creative ways of describing her pain and discomfort.

ME: Thanks for that graphic depiction. It will haunt my dreams tonight. And good news, I'm no longer hungry, so that takes care of missing our dinner date before the movie.

CHARLOTTE: You're welcome, my friend. I know you were looking forward to our Taron Egerton perv-fest, but alas, it must be postponed. Next Friday work for you?

My shoulders slump. I really was looking forward to spending some quality screen time with the dreamboat that is Mr. Egerton.

ME: I hate you and your moody reproductive organs. Until next week then. Kisses.

No longer having a reason to hang around at the office, I shut down my computer, slide my feet back into my heels, slip my bag over my shoulder, and stride out like a woman on a mission.

Let it be noted—there is no mission. And I have nowhere to go but home to my empty apartment to sulk about the lack of supersized man candy in my life this evening. I. Am. Pathetic.

Rhett

I WINK AT THE BARTENDER AS SHE LEANS farther forward than necessary to slide my beer across the timber expanse separating us. "Thanks, sugar."

The tip of her pink tongue glides across her full bottom lip. "You're welcome, handsome."

A blonde stripper shakes her plentiful arse in front of Simon's face. Laughter bubbles up my throat. Simon is pressing his torso back in his seat, trying to get as far away from her as possible; it's fucking hilarious. And I'm immediately pleased with myself for organising this buck's night for him.

A grin splits my face as I drop down into the seat beside him. "There is a gorgeous woman rubbing herself all over you, and you're cringing ... That's the wrong response, man."

Simon's head snaps to me. "You are a sick son of a bitch, Rhett. Jessie is going to go nuts if she finds out about this." His eyes bug out of his head. "Look at this, look." His eyes drop down to indicate the red smear on the collar of his white dress shirt. "There's lipstick on it!"

My grin transforms into a smirk. "I know, but it's my duty as your best friend and best man to get you in as much shit as possible."

"Well, you've certainly lived up to your obligations over the past fifteen years, you prick."

"And you've loved every minute of it. You would have died of boredom without me in your life, and you know it," I tell him with a nudge to his ribs.

He shakes his head, and finally, having had enough of the stripper's attention, he leans forward and whispers in her ear. She instantly straightens, moving away from him, and glares at me. *Me.* What the fuck did he just say to her? Before I can ask, she slaps me across the face and storms—as much as one can storm in stripper heels—away from the corner of the bar we've taken up.

I glare at Simon. "What did you say?"

The smug bastard shrugs. "I did what I had to do. Now, if you'll excuse me." He plants his feet then stands, dusting imaginary lint off his shirt. "I'm going to find some club soda to get this shit off my collar before I go home to my fiancée."

Three steps into the abandonment of his own buck's party, he looks back to me and calls out, "Thanks, dick-face. And I think that new cream should really help the rash on your balls. Just don't forget to apply it three times a day."

Conveniently, the cute bartender I was planning on taking home is standing close enough to hear my once best friend's implication that I have an STD. That asshole.

Eight or nine drinks later, I stumble into a cab —alone.

Jesus Christ. What the fuck is that?
 CLUNK   *THWACK*   *THWACK* *THWACK*

PINK BITS

For the love of GOD! My hand shoots to my throbbing skull. The sound on the other side of the wall continues, and with each thwack, my brain flinches.

I sit up and instantly regret the sudden movement as my stomach rolls. Another thwack vibrates through the wall behind my bed, and my eyes squeeze shut. What the hell is she doing over there?

I'm drowning in sweat—stupid bloody air con. Once the urge to throw up eases, I gingerly swing my legs over the side of my bed, pressing the soles of my feet to the floor. Only when I'm sure I'm not going to empty the contents of my stomach all over the carpet do I stand. My head spins, and I press my hand to the wall to steady myself, then make my way over to the air-conditioner unit above my drawers.

Glaring at it, I reach up and give it a little love tap. Nothing. I do it again, a little less lovingly. Still nothing. Frustration boils under my skin until another loud thwack fills the room, and an idea blossoms in the pits of my hungover brain.

Striding down the hall with purpose, I head straight to my front door. Wrapping my fingers around the handle, I yank it open and stalk towards my quirky little neighbour's apartment. I bang on it with a heavy hand to make sure she can hear me over the sound of whatever the hell she's doing in there.

I only cease when the door swings away from my pounding fist and I'm met with a dishevelled little psycho clutching a hammer. I blink at her. What the fuck—

"Rhett?" she squeaks. "Where are your pants?"

My gaze drops down to my cock, now half-erect due to the sexy little number in front of me. A vision of this gorgeous creature standing just like that at the foot of my bed while offering to play handywoman for me plays out in my mind. "Umm ..." I shake my head and wince at the movement. "It's not important," I mutter as I shove past her on my way inside the apartment.

The cool air inside sends a chill scattering over my skin. Spotting a plush grey couch, I smile and head over to my new hibernation zone. I grab a few of the throw pillows, toss them on the floor, then snatch a particularly cosy-looking one back out of the pile I just discarded. I squish it a few times to make sure it's a keeper, then wrap my arm under it as I lie down, snuggling into the surprisingly soft fabric of Neighbour Girl's couch.

Just as I've closed my eyes, she appears. "What are you doing? And where are your pants?"

I pop one annoyed eye open to glare at her.

"What does it look like I'm doing? I'm going to sleep. And pants are overrated."

"Pants are overrated," she mumbles under her breath. And I think she's taken the hint to leave me alone, but I'm wrong. "No, I—this is weird. Even for me, this is weird. *I* wouldn't even do this. I barely know you. Do you even know my name? Why are you naked in my apartment at five in the morning? No, wait, the time doesn't matter. Why are you in my apartment? And why are you naked?"

Opening both my eyes to give her the full power of my sleep-deprived, hungover glare, I spell out what should be quite obvious. "I'm in your apartment because *you* woke me up, and my air conditioner is broken, and it's hot as fucking hell at my place. A fact that I was oblivious to when I was asleep but became very aware of after you started trying to knock out the wall that divides our apartments with that fucking hammer."

She blinks down at me several times. "I see."

I nod. "I knew you would. Now, if you'll kindly stop staring, I'd like to go back to sleep."

She does not stop staring. I can't sleep when someone is looking at me. It's creepy as fuck. So, I stare back at her, then slowly raise a brow when she makes no move to leave. "Did I miss something?" I ask.

She licks her lips and wrinkles her forehead. "Do you even know my name?" she asks tentatively.

Uh, shit. I rack my brain in a vain attempt to come up with it. The look on my face must give me away, because she draws her shoulders back and mutters, "That's what I thought."

When she doesn't say anything else, I release a heavy sigh and gingerly sit up. "Look, it's not like we've been officially introduced or anything, but I know who you are. You're Neighbour Girl; you've lived next door for the last four years. You have one friend you always hang out with who laughs like a hyena. I'm guessing no boyfriend because I've never seen a man here, and—"

Her hand flies out and covers my mouth. "Okay, I get it. You don't have to tell me how sad my life is."

I'm tempted to lick her palm just to see how she tastes, but that would be inappropriate.

After dropping her hand from my face, she holds it out in offering to me. "I'm Reagan."

I glance at her outstretched palm then take it, wrapping my much larger one around her delicate one. "Rhett."

She nods, seemingly pleased with herself. "I already knew your name. Girls scream it so loud it practically makes my bedroom wall quake in orgasm along with them."

The hell did she just say?

My jaw pops open, and I wait for her to attempt to take back her words, to blush, to do anything but stare at me like she didn't just say that out loud. But she doesn't. I'm still clutching her hand in mine, and I notice how soft her skin is. The pad of my thumb strokes across the pulse point in her wrist, and she smiles.

That semi I was sporting when I arrived inflates to straight-up hard-on as dimples pop in her cheeks. Then her eyes flash downwards, and she drops the hammer she was still holding. Glass shatters. I release her hand to cradle my skull as my brain tries to burst through my eyeballs at the god-awful sound.

"Fuck," I moan.

"Shit, my coffee table!" she yells. Then she crouches down in front of me and asks, "Are you okay?" Her palm comes into contact with my forehead. "You're awfully warm."

Her position gives me a bird's-eye view straight down her loose top. And—sweet Jesus—she's not wearing a bra. If I didn't want to die this very second, I'd be hitting on her like there was no tomorrow. My throat thickens, and so does my cock.

All of a sudden, she's no longer touching my forehead because she's plastered to the wall on the far side of the room. Her hand rises and points—to. My. Dick. I drop my gaze to it, too. "Uh, sorry?"

She shakes her head back and forth slowly, then licks her pink lips. "Does it have a name?"

My brows pop. "What?"

Reagan blinks. Her big blue eyes slowly travel up my body until they come to meet mine. She repeats her question. "Does it have a name? Your penis," she clarifies—as if she had to.

I gape. "My dick." I tilt my head. "You— What —" I close my eyes. Am I still asleep? Surely that's what's happening here; I dreamt this whole situation up. I nod to myself then open my eyes again. Nope, she's still there. No hint of embarrassment on her pretty face at all. And she's still pointing.

My cock twitches as if waving to her, and I wrap my hand over him protectively. "He does, but it's personal."

She frowns and lowers her hand. "Oh, okay." She shrugs but stays stuck to the wall.

I've had a hell of a lot of different reactions to the size of my dick, but this is new. Not once has anyone asked if he had a name. Or run away from him that far and fast. I observe her curiously. I've always known Neighbour Girl was on the quirky side, but this?

It would appear she is observing me just as

closely as I am her. Those big doe eyes of hers rove over me. Inquisitiveness glints in their depths as she continues to stare.

For the first time in my life, I feel self-conscious. I sneer. *Self-conscious?* Ugh, I don't fucking think so. I'm fucking glorious, and so is my dick.

Chapter Two

Reagan

I know I'm being rude, but I can't look away. It's impolite to stare. I'm vaguely aware that I've slipped into full-blown creeper territory, but holy shit, that thing is out of this world. I swallow hard as it bobs against Rhett's tight stomach.

How is this even my reality right now? Sexy men do not turn up at my apartment door at five a.m., naked, and throw themselves on my couch to settle in for a nap. This isn't normal behaviour. Nothing normal ever happens to me, but this feels next-level.

He's staring back at me, waiting for me to say something else. At least, I think he is. So, I bite down on the edge of my bottom lip, trying to think of something, anything, to say. "I'm not a creeper, it's just... well... you're very well-endowed. It's quite shocking, really. I'm a little stuck on it."

Rhett blinks back at me, then a tiny grin lifts the corner of his mouth. "Um yeah, he's impressive. But I've never quite had a reaction like this before."

"Oh, I suffer from a debilitating case of awkwardness. I've gotten used to it, but other people find it kind of jarring." I shrug. It's the best explanation I can give.

His grin widens until it's covering his entire gorgeous face. "Debilitating awkwardness? That's a new one. Normally I get, *Oh that thing's huge. Fancy a blow job instead?*" He mimics the high-pitched tone of a pub bunny's voice, then covers his mouth and flutters his strangely long—for a man's—eyelashes.

I snort. "You're not serious."

That sexy grin morphs into an unimpressed scowl, all traces of humour gone. "I wish I weren't. But I am. Apparently there is such a thing as *too big*."

My nose and forehead crinkle. "Too big? Women think your penis is too big? I mean, yeah, it's big—like, really big—but I wouldn't say *too* big." Then I think on it for a moment. "Well, I guess it depends on what you're wanting to do with it as to whether it's too big. It's all about perspective, you know?" As I talk, a wide grin stretches across his gorgeous face.

Arching a brow, he asks, "Perspective? And what would you do with my dick, Reagan?"

I scratch my head. "I don't know. You'd have to give me time to ponder on it. I haven't come into contact with anything like that before, so it would require brainstorming, I think."

A rich belly laugh fills the room as Rhett throws himself back into the couch cushions, laughing his arse off at my expense. Now this is something I'm used to.

Crossing my arms over my chest, I glare at him. "Are you done?"

It takes him a few minutes to pull himself together, and when he does, he smiles at me—a genuine, happy smile, making my defences drop just a little.

"You're one weird chick, but I like it," he says.

I have to consider if I want to take this as a compliment or an insult. Finally, I decide it's a compliment. "Normal is overrated," I tell him, repeating his line about pants.

He nods. "I dig it. Nice ink." He gestures to my shoulder piece with his chin as he speaks. "You like roses?"

"I like all flowers," I tell him, then realise I've unglued myself from the wall and somehow made my way back into the middle of the lounge room.

"Shit," I mutter when a sharp pain sears through my foot. Looking down, I see blood pooling under my left foot. Nausea rolls through me. My head spins rapidly, and sparks fly in my vision. *Oh no, here we go ...*

A fraction of a second before I hit the glass-covered floor, Rhett's big arms wrap around me, and he tugs me into his hard, defined, NAKED chest. Our bodies crash back into the couch, sending it screeching across the tiles from our combined weight.

I'm somewhat aware that I should be extracting myself from his hold, seeing as he isn't wearing any clothes, but I'm too dizzy to even try. I'm a limp noodle in this gorgeous man's arms, and he's anything but. Somehow, when Rhett rescued me from certain face mutilation, our bodies got so tangled that I'm splayed across his lap. And his penis is now lodged between my breasts, poking its head out as if to say, *Hello.*

My head sways a little, and I'm no longer sure if it's from seeing the blood or from being this close to *it*. I wish he'd told me its name; I feel rude just staring at it and not knowing.

"... lot of blood. I think you might need stitches," Rhett says.

I blink slowly then rotate my head so I can look up into his face. "What?"

He's holding my bloodied foot in the air,

examining it closely. "It looks pretty deep. I think you're going to need stitches."

"Oh," I say, as if this is perfectly okay when it is anything but. I do not do hospitals. I do not do blood, or needles, or any of the other shit involved in what he just said. Turning my face forward again, I rest my now sweaty forehead against his firm thigh, close my eyes, and take several deep, calming breaths.

I've barely begun my internal calm-your-tits speech when his thigh goes rock solid. My eyes pop open. "Can you chill for like five minutes? I'm in the middle of a crisis here. I can feel your lack of chill, and it's making it hard for me to remain calm." Every damn inch of him is statue-like by the time I finish my request.

"Uh, yeah, that's not going to happen when my cock is nestled between your fun bags and you're blowing nice warm breaths over his head like you're about to show him some love."

My head rolls to the side, and I peer up at him with one eye. "Seriously? I'm about to bleed out on my couch and you think I want to give you a BJ?" What is wrong with him?

Rhett frowns. "Bleed out? That's a little dramatic. You're going to need stitches, not a funeral director."

With herculean effort, I move my arms to the

outside of his thigh and push my torso up so I come eye to eye with him. "I am not dramatic."

It would have been a much bolder statement had my arms been stable beneath me and had I not just caught sight of the blood running down my ankle and pooling at the back of my bent knee. Lightness fills my head, and I feel it droop as my arms give out and the world around me goes black.

Rhett

THERE COMES A TIME IN EVERY MAN'S LIFE WHEN he must ask himself, *how did I end up here?* This is my moment: sitting naked on a practical stranger's couch with her sprawled over me, her face mashed against my fully erect cock as I hold one of her legs up in the air in an attempt to slow the blood flow from her foot. Oh yes, and let's not forget that she's currently unconscious.

Using my free hand, I slide the curtain of blonde hair that escaped from her bun-thing off her face. She's white as a sheet, and when I press my palm to her forehead, I feel how clammy she is. Shit. I need to get her to a hospital, but I'm naked.

How do I get myself into these situations? Given, this particular one is a first, but still, how?

As smoothly as possible, I slide out from underneath her, keeping her injured foot elevated. Then I notice the blood now soaked into the cushions of her nice couch. Double shit. I lower her ankle to lean it on the armrest, then survey the ground before stepping back. Last thing I need is to stand on a piece of glass, too.

Gripping my hips, I stare at her. Her face is squished into the cushion, and her mouth is open. It looks like a fucking crime scene in here. My hand slips off my hip, and it's because it's covered in blood. Great. It looks like I tried to kill her. Somehow, I don't think my reason for being here would help my case—*I swear, Officer, I was just coming over to take a nap.*

Fuck it, I have to fix this. Sleep will wait, but this headache needs to be dealt with now. It takes me less than a minute to get the layout of Reagan's apartment figured out. It's very similar to my own, only nicer.

I rummage through her bathroom cabinets and find some Advil, bandages, and sterile wipes. They'll do just nicely. Glancing at her shower on my way out, I decide it's probably a good idea to jump in real quick, seeing as I look like an axe murderer at rush hour.

Adjusting the temperature, I slide in and soap up with her girly rosewood body wash and remove all traces of her blood from my skin. This stuff is actually pretty nice; it smells delicate and enticing. I quickly rinse off and grab the first towel I can find—it's sunshine yellow. I swiftly dry off then wrap it around my hips and pick up my medical supplies.

When I stride into the lounge room, Reagan is no longer horizontal. You'd think that would be a good thing, but the look on her face says it's really not. Tears shine in her baby blues, and I rush to her, mindful of the glass. "Hey, it's okay. You're okay," I tell her.

She shakes her head, and big fat tears roll down her cheeks, wrinkled from being smooshed into the couch. "I forgot I hurt my foot, and tried to stand up, and stood on another-piece-of-glass-and-now-it's-stuck-in-my-foot-and-I'm-going-to-die ..." she wails, folding herself into my body as I sit.

My arm automatically curls around the eccentric woman beside me, and I hold her, stroking her arm in comfort. "You're not going to die, Reagan. I won't let you."

Her big blue eyes connect with mine. "Promise?"

I don't even hesitate. "I promise."

Keeping our eyes locked, I reach down and wrap my free hand around her ankle. "Close your eyes, beautiful," I instruct. I don't want her to pass out again. Then, I lift her foot towards me while sliding my arm out from under her and guide her to lie back. "Just breathe, Reagan."

Her eyes screw shut, and she does as I say. Shifting my attention to her foot, I cringe. A large piece of glass sticks out of the side. Thick, sticky blood runs down her leg and drips onto the floor. It's so fucking gross. The metallic smell makes my stomach roll, and I have to look away for a second to get my shit together.

"I'm going to pull out the glass, Reagan, then I'm going to take you to the hospital." My fingers slip twice before I'm able to get a good grip on the shard. I don't wait for her to respond. Holding it firmly, I pull it out in one fluid motion, then press the towel that's around my waist to the area.

I expect a scream or something from her, but she stays silent. Peeking back at her face, I realise it's because she's out cold. It's probably better that way. Snatching up the bandages I found in the bathroom, I wrap one around her foot and secure it with some medical tape.

Sliding out from under her, I crouch by her side. "Reagan," I whisper as I stroke her cold cheek. She stirs. "I'm going back to my place real quick to get some clothes and my keys. I'll be right back. Don't go anywhere."

She mumbles something incoherent, and I don't think she'll be moving off this couch without my help anytime soon.

I take off back to my apartment, but not before putting a piece of the medical tape over the latch of Reagan's apartment door to make sure I can get back in. Once inside my place, I duck into my spare room and grab a pair of pants and the first tee I find. My keys, however, are not as easily found.

Then, I have a light bulb moment and check the pockets of the jeans I was wearing last night—success! Wrapping my fist around them, I snatch my phone off the kitchen counter and slide my feet into my shoes on the way out the door.

Reagan is where I left her, but she's awake now. When I walk in, she stares at me like I've grown a second head, then bursts out laughing. Shit, maybe she's lost so much blood she's delirious? The closer I get to her, the harder she laughs, until tears slide down the sides of her now rosy cheeks.

I raise my brows. "What's so funny?" She could at least let me in on the joke.

She raises a shaking finger. "Your shirt," she snorts.

Fuck. My. Life.

I grabbed the tee my sister gave me for my birthday last month. It says, *Sexy and I Mow It,* with a picture of a stick man pushing a lawnmower. I roll my eyes at Reagan. "It's not that funny. I mowed my sister's lawn for her once—just once—and it was really fucking hot, and I had to take my shirt off, and her friends were over. And yeah, I may have made the joke to one of them who was drooling a little." I shrug. "I didn't even look at what I was putting on. I was just trying to be quick."

"Thanks," she says, smiling brightly, "and I like the shirt."

"Come on. Let's get you some medical attention," I say with an outstretched hand. She takes it and I help her sit. "You want to change your clothes first, or want a bra or something?"

An adorable wrinkle forms between her brows. "A bra? No. I'm in pain; why would I want to inflict more discomfort on myself right now? Let's just get this over with."

I grin. "Suits me fine; I'm not complaining." In fact, I really like that she doesn't want to doll herself up, or some shit like that, before leaving the house.

"I'm sure you're not, you perv. Don't think I

didn't see you lookin' earlier," she mumbles as I help her stand, then wrap my arm around her slim waist and take most of her weight.

I deliberately look down her top, which is easy since she's tiny next to my six foot two. "I wasn't trying to hide it. And it's only fair since you spent a solid ten minutes staring at my dick."

She playfully shoves my side as I escort her out the door and down to the basement garage, leading her to my truck. She leans on its side while I fish out my keys and unlock my baby, then I scoop her up and deposit her inside.

"I could have climbed up," she mutters.

"I know, but you would have hurt your foot. It's no big deal."

Fifteen minutes later, I slide into a park by the emergency entrance. "I'll help you out," I tell her and jog around the front of the truck before she tries to climb down on her own.

Her door is already open, and she's about to slide out when I wrap my arms around her little waist. "I told you I'd help you."

She stares into my eyes as I slowly lower her to the ground.

"I'm okay; you've done enough. Really, I can take it from here. You should go now." She says all this with a pleasant smile plastered on her face. And it's fake as fuck.

I scrutinise her for a minute longer. "What are you planning?"

Her eyes widen. "What? Nothing. I'm going to go in and get fixed up good as new, and then I'll call my dad to come get me. No hidden plans here."

"Really? 'Cause your eyes keep darting to that taxi rank over there, and I'm having flashbacks of you burying your face in my crotch to process the fact that you need stitches. So, I'm thinking you have a plan of escape and you're trying to get rid of me."

Her smile falters. "Damn it. I'm such a shitty liar. I really need to work on that."

I'm about to release my hold when her body tips to the side. I tighten my grip. "Whoa there, come on, drama queen. I'll hold your hand the whole time, okay?"

She swallows. "Uh no, you don't need to do that. Nobody wants to see what's about to go down in there."

I hook a finger under her chin and tilt her head up when she refuses to meet my gaze. "And what's going to go down?"

Reagan releases a deep breath. "A whole lot of crazy you are not prepared to handle. I should call my daddy," she says and gnaws on her bottom lip.

At this point, it's hard to keep a straight face. "More crazy than our morning so far, you mean?"

Finally, a fraction of a real smile quirks her full lips. "Yeah, probably."

Chapter Three

Rhett

What the actual fuck am I seeing right now?

I blink several times then wriggle my fingers. Well, I try to wriggle my fingers.

Reagan has my hand in a death grip as she shrieks, "WHY ME, GOD?"

My ears are actually ringing. "Calm down, woman. They haven't even touched you yet."

Her chest heaves as she pulls air into her lungs in sharp, harsh pants. "I am calm, you dick-hole! This is all your fault. You did this to me. You cut me!" Her rabid eyes bounce around the small sterile cubicle.

She already tried to do a runner but collapsed two feet in, presumably from the numerous cuts on her foot. I scooped her up, and I've been holding her like this for the last ten minutes. My arms lock around her middle a little tighter. "Jesus, you weren't lying about the crazy."

"You did not just call me crazy! You're crazy. You, you made me come here. This is your fault." Her rambling would be cute if she hadn't been doing it since we walked through the doors.

Seriously, we crossed the threshold, and her mouth started moving and hasn't stopped since. She's even more pale than she was when we were back at her apartment, and sweat is gathering at her temples, across her nape, and down her slender neck. I'm struck with the urge to kiss her there, right in the curve where her neck meets her shoulder. Just rest my lips there to soothe her.

Jesus, her crazy is rubbing off on me. I shake my head and ask the doctor, "What's taking so long?"

He smiles, clearly way too amused by the rabid banshee in my lap. "Oh, just waiting on another set of hands. Won't be too long."

I nod. Right. Another set of hands can't hurt, even though there are already two nurses hovering in the corner. Can't we get this show on the road? The curtain parts and another doctor steps inside. His eyes land on Reagan and he smiles at her. "Hello, sweetheart. It's been a long time. What have you done to yourself?"

Her bottom lip trembles, and she points to her foot wrapped in the bloodied bandage. "He cut me," she sobs.

I roll my eyes. "I didn't cut her. She dropped a hammer on her glass coffee table, then stood on the shards when she was staring at my—" I cut myself off. They don't need all the details.

The guy nods, then extends a weathered hand to me. "Jim. I've been Reagan's doctor since she was a child."

"Rhett. I'm her neighbour."

After releasing my hand, he clasps his in front of him and crouches down in front of us. "Honey, you need to calm down. I'll get the nurse to bring you a Valium, then we'll take a look at the damage."

Reagan nods, finally fucking silent.

When Jim returns to standing, Reagan's eyes zero in on the blood-stained bandage. The longer she stares at it, the looser her stiff body becomes in my arms. "Reagan?" I question, cupping her jaw with my hand, swivelling it so I can look into her eyes. They're cloudy and her cheeks have a slightly green tinge to them.

"So much blood," she mumbles, then her head jerks out of my hold as she vomits all over both of us. And promptly passes out, again.

The nurses scurry to clean up the mess, and Doctor

Jim jumps to action. "Right, let's have a look at this while she's out," he says to the first doctor. Glancing at one of the nurses, he instructs her to get something. I'm not sure what, as I'm too busy trying to hold my own vomit back. I've always been a sympathetic vomiter.

I clench my jaw as nausea grips my stomach. "Ah, Doc, I'm going to have to lay her on that there bed before I add to the—" I retch before I can finish my sentence.

Thirty minutes later, I've showered in the patients' bathrooms and am wearing a pair of blue scrubs. Reagan's been moved to another cubicle—a clean one, thank god. I'm grateful for the strong scent of hospital-grade cleaning products filling my nostrils as I walk past our previous one.

Reagan's still passed out when I enter the small area we've been designated, the doctor hovering by her side. "Umm, Doc, is she supposed to be out still?"

"We gave her a little something to keep her under while we cleaned the wound and sutured it. We have administered local anaesthetic to the area, but with Reagan, it's best she not be conscious for such things."

I nod along as he explains. Makes sense to knock her crazy arse out. She'd probably kick the doctors in the face sooner than let them look at the cuts.

I'm told she can leave an hour after she comes back around if her hysteria has calmed down. I drag a chair up to the side of her bed and wait.

Reagan

My head lulls to the side, and I squint. My surroundings are weird. I look around fully and realise I'm in a hospital bed. Then, my eyes land on him.

I swallow hard as the memory of my morning comes crashing down on me. Holy-baked-not-fried-potato-chips. He saw my crazy. All my crazy. My hot-as-sin neighbour—who I may have fantasised about a few (hundred) times—saw me at my ultimate level of crazy. Kill. Me. Now.

An audible groan leaves my lips, and I smack my hand over my mouth to hush the sound. Rhett's eyes fly open and lock on my face.

I am beyond mortified. Then, he smiles.

"Hey there, crazy girl," he says with a smirk. "How you feelin'?"

Is it wrong that I want to both slap and kiss that smirk off his face?

When I don't answer his question, he shuffles to the edge of the chair he's sitting on and rests his elbows on the side of my bed. His eyes rake over me, from the top of my head right down to my toes.

Wait, what the hell am I wearing? I pluck at the offending garment covering my upper body. Scrubs?

"You threw up on us, then I threw up on us," Rhett explains, cringing.

For the love of God. Can this day get any worse?

"I recall. But I don't remember putting this on." I pluck at the top I'm wearing again. "I would never—and I mean *never*—willingly wear scrubs."

Rhett's lips twitch. "You'd prefer to stay in your manky, puke-covered clothes?"

And that's when it dawns on my sluggish brain that Rhett, too, is wearing scrubs. But unlike me, he looks like a sexy doctor from *Grey's Anatomy*.

"I'd prefer to be naked than wear these." I sniff. Before he can comment, my brain chooses that moment to filter through his explanation of the scrubs. I narrow my eyes. "Did you say that *you* threw up on us?"

His smile falls. "Umm, yeah. I have a weak stomach when it comes to that kind of thing. I've been a sympathetic spewer since I was a kid when my baby sister would vomit up her milk; I'd be there, right beside her, chucking up my breakfast."

Right. Well, that's disgusting.

"You didn't answer me before. How are you feeling?"

Glancing down at my pristinely wrapped foot, I shrug. "I'm fine."

Rhett arches a brow. "Just like that? From crazy to cruisy with the flip of a coin?"

I shrug again. "I can't see the... you know... anymore. It's a visual thing."

"But you were fine on the car ride over here. You didn't turn into a nutcase until we walked in the doors."

Clearing my throat, I explain, "The bandages were clean when you drove me here. But by the time we got inside, the red stuff had seeped through, and bam—welcome to Crazytown."

"I think I get it. It's like me with the vomit, but you go crazy at the sight of blood."

I nod. "Yeppers. Now, can we go? I hate being in here."

"Gotta wait to see the doc first, then I'll take you home," he tells me.

I wonder why he hung around, especially after the cray-cray came out to play. I want to ask him, but at the same time, I'm content to just sit here in silence for a few minutes. This day has been one I'll never forget for the rest of my life, as much as I want to. And it's only ten a.m.

Hobbling into my apartment, I glance over my shoulder at Rhett who's standing in the doorway. "You coming in?"

He scratches his temple. "Do you want me to?"

I shrug. I had just assumed he would, seeing as he barged in here this morning like he owned the place. "Umm, I guess? I don't know. I mean ..." I'm stumped for what to say. Hell yes, I want him to come in, but this is all so strange. I'm not sure what the appropriate response is here.

He's so damn pretty I want to lick his face. But if I said that out loud, he definitely wouldn't come in. And he'd never try to sleep naked on my couch again. I gnaw on my bottom lip. I really want to call Char and ask her what I should say, but my phone is in the lounge room still, and I can't just make him wait in my doorway while I scurry off to phone a friend.

"Look, it's fine. I can go home. But maybe you should give me your number so I can check up on you, and you can call me if you need anything, yeah?"

My eyes shoot to his. "No, it's okay. You can come in. I'm just, well, I told you, I'm super awkward."

He takes a step inside, then closes the door behind him. "If you want me to go, that's totally fine, Reagan. Don't feel like you have to invite me in," he says while running his calloused hand through his messy hair. "You were right; this is my fault. If I hadn't forced my way in here this morning, none of this would have happened. I was just so tired and really fucking hungover—it seemed like a great plan." His shoulders rise in apology, and he drops his gaze to the floor.

I swing my body around to face him using the horrendous crutches the hospital supplied me with. "Don't apologise. If you didn't come over, I never would have had the nerve to introduce myself to you, and we'd still be strangers."

His eyes lift to meet mine. "That's true. But you'd still be in one piece."

With a roll of my eyes, I swivel back around and continue hobbling into my lounge room, only to freeze at the sight before me.

It's clean. No glass, no blood, nothing.

I can feel the heat of Rhett's body at my back.

"What happened? I don't understand." I crane

my neck to look up at him as an impish grin spreads across his face.

He scratches the back of his neck as he says, "I rang my sister. I didn't want you to freak out all over again, trying to clean up the mess. So, yeah, I made a call to the most OCD woman I know, and she did her thing."

A lump of emotion forms in my throat; he's so thoughtful. I totally would have lost my shit again if I'd had to face the crime scene. Licking my parched lips, I wait for his eyes to meet mine. "Thank you," I whisper, unable to make my voice any louder for fear of it breaking.

Rhett shrugs his wide shoulders, his grin having morphed into a megawatt smile. "It's no problem. I'm just glad I could do something to make it better for you." His warm hands slide around my hips as he leans forward. "Is this okay?"

I'm stunned at the contact and how my body hums with delight at the small gesture. "More than okay," I breathe. I want him to kiss me so badly my lips tingle.

He tilts his head in a small nod, then applies pressure to my hips, urging me forward. I'm instantly confused. I thought he was making a move, not guiding me into the lounge room.

Once in front of my gloriously clean couch, he

turns me around and pushes my hips back until I sit. Then, in one swift move, he lifts my legs and swings them up onto it. I stare at him—like really stare. He's so sweet and chivalrous. Such a contradiction to the naked man who barged in here at the arse-crack of dawn to take a nap on my couch.

Chapter Four

Reagan

Rhett doesn't leave, instead taking up residence on my floral velvet daybed opposite me. He is way too big for it, but he looks comfy enough with his arms tucked behind his head as he lounges.

I flick on the TV and pretend to watch it. I'm not even sure what channel it's on—it could be playing porn for all the attention I'm paying to it. I can't look away from him. This is all so surreal.

"You're staring again," he says.

"This whole day has been one bizarre event after another. I'm just processing."

"Can you process while not staring at me?" he asks, turning his head to eye me.

I shrug. "Maybe, but you're part of it. So I'm processing you, too."

He rolls onto his side, propping his head up with

his arm, keeping eye contact as he speaks. "I think I'm the one who should be processing. This has been, by far, the strangest day on record for me. From your reaction to my dick, to the shitshow at the hospital ..." He shakes his head. "Mind fuck." He uses his free hand to mime an explosion coming from his brain.

Snorting, I turn the TV off, then correct him. "Uh no. You're the one who showed up at my place—naked, I might add—to take a nap. Who does that? We didn't even know each other six hours ago."

"Pfft, you woke me up! I was sleeping like a fucking baby until someone"—he raises his brows pointedly at me—"tried to take down the wall between our places. What were you doing with that hammer anyway?"

I shift a little and avert my gaze. "I don't know what you're talking about." His eyes bore into me, and I squirm, refusing to meet his inquisitive examination.

"Reagan, I can just go look for myself, you know. You'd be too slow to stop me, so you might as well just spit it out."

"Hmph, fine," I grumble but keep my focus on my pretty, pale purple toenails. "I couldn't sleep, so I thought I'd do some remodelling."

"Remodelling. I see."

I don't like his tone. I bet he thinks I'm incapable

of doing it myself. Typical male. I slide my gaze towards him, but he's gone. I didn't even hear him get up. My eyes widen in panic as I swing my feet to the floor, and I wince in pain at the slight pressure on my injured foot.

"Don't bother coming after me; I've already found it. There's no sense in you hurting yourself trying to stop me." His voice comes from the short hallway that leads to my bedroom.

I drop my head back in defeat. Damn him. He has some serious ninja-like stealth abilities.

A few minutes later, Rhett emerges, an amused smirk in place. "Not happy with the layout of your closet, huh?"

Glaring at his stupidly gorgeous face, I cross my arms under my boobs. "No, I wasn't. I need more room for my shoes and more hanging space."

He nods as he approaches me. Crouching down at my feet, he lifts them, swings them back up onto the couch, then hands me a light pink tank top. I frown, and he smiles shyly. "You were bitching about the scrubs, and this was on the end of your bed." He shrugs and moves his right hand back to my ankle. "You should keep your foot up," he instructs. "It will help with the swelling."

"Okay." I swallow, the intensity of his gaze making my heart beat faster. I blink at him several times then shift my focus to the tank he handed me. He makes me feel so weird, all twisty inside. I yank my top off and throw it to the floor, then slip the tank over my head. He's so thoughtful.

"Sweet Jesus," Rhett breathes, and my eyes find his again, but they're locked on my breasts.

"Something wrong?" I ask.

He releases a slow, controlled breath. "You're not wearing a bra, Reagan." His eyes finally meet mine. "You just flashed me your amazing tits."

"Oh," is all I can say. Holy shit. He's going to think I'm a whore. "I haven't had sex in ages!" I blurt. His eyes widen, and I try to explain myself. "I'm not trying to get into your pants or anything, is what I mean. I... um... shit. I didn't even think about it. You gave me the clean, non-nasty tank, and I really did hate that other top, so I just changed it." I shrug pathetically. "Sorry," I mumble.

"Don't ever be sorry for who you are, Reagan. Besides, I didn't think you were trying to seduce me or anything. After only half a day with you, I'm beginning to realise you just do and say whatever pops into your head."

I nod. "I do. It's an illness. Not everybody is as chill about it as you. Although, I wasn't apologising for being me; I was apologising for flashing you."

He frowns. "Oh, well, don't be sorry for that

either." His thumb grazes over the ankle bone of my injured foot. "Doc said you should stay off it for at least a week before you try getting around again. Will that be a problem with your job?"

I shake my head. "No, I can work from home."

"Good," he murmurs, his thumb still lightly tracing the contours of my foot. "I can come check on you each morning, make sure you've got breakfast and supplies for the day, if you want."

Hazel eyes bore into mine, and I'm caught in a daze. "Yeah, that'd be nice." Truth be told, I could get Char to come stay with me and help, but she doesn't look like Rhett. So, I push that thought away.

The answering smile he gives me says I definitely made the right choice. That and the butterflies swarming in my chest. I grin back.

Could Rhett be the one guy who doesn't find my awkward nature overbearing?

Rhett

THIS CHICK IS UNLIKE ANY I'VE EVER MET. I'M A "hit it and quit it" kind of guy with no need for conversation or bonding. I only put in the time needed to secure myself a warm body for the night. But Reagan is different. I want to help her, feed her, hang out with her. And I'm not even thinking about banging her.

Okay, that's a lie. I'm totally thinking about having sex with her. It's really freaking hard not to stare at her tits. Especially when I'm this close to her and she just changed in front of me. And ... now I'm doing exactly what I was trying not to do: staring at them.

"They're pretty impressive, huh?"

My eyes snap to hers, expecting her to be pissed or something, but a genuine smile lights her features. I should have known she wouldn't care. "Umm, yeah, they're pretty fucking awesome."

"And they're real," she says, squeezing one in her hand.

Goddamn, *she's* unreal. Before I can say anything in response, her stomach growls. Loudly. "Hungry?"

She nods. "Yeah, I haven't eaten today. There's food in the fridge. I got groceries on my way home last night." She tries to swing her legs around, but I stop her.

"No, I'll get it. Stay here."

Her apartment is the same layout as mine, so her kitchen is just beyond the lounge area. In her fridge, I find all the fixings I'll need to make us some sandwiches. While I throw them together, I check out her space. The benches are shiny hot pink laminate, the cupboard doors are deep plum purple, and the splash zone is like a chalkboard with notes and scribbles here and there.

My kitchen looks the same as it did the day I moved in: simple black benchtop with white cupboard doors. Reagan's is much cooler. *Maybe I should do something with mine?*

Sliding the two sandwiches onto a couple of plates, I carry them back into the lounge room and hand hers over. Taking a seat opposite her, I watch her from the corner of my eye as she takes a bite, grinning when she spots me watching her.

"It's good. Thank you."

I smirk. "I know."

We're eating in companionable silence when she speaks up. "Did you know flamingo tongues were a common delicacy in Roman feasts back in the day?"

I pause, the bite I just took falling from my mouth back to my plate as I gape at her. "What?"

"True fact; the Romans had some freakishly disgusting tastes."

Suddenly, my sandwich doesn't look so appealing. I glance at it, and back to Reagan, who is still munching away happily on hers, then put my plate with the remainder of my lunch on the floor beside me.

"Where did you pull that little gem of knowledge from?" I ask while crossing my arms behind my head as I lie back on the couch.

"It's what I do. I am the queen of random facts," Reagan says from the couch opposite me.

"Aha, so you just like collecting weird little bits of information for fun? Or to gross people out while they're trying to eat?" I joke.

Her blue eyes widen and shoot to my plate on the floor with the remains of my sandwich. "Shit, I'm sorry. I didn't mean to turn you off your food. I'm hopeless. Small talk is not my thing. I always say the wrong thing. I'm such a loser."

"Whoa, that's not what I meant. It's fine, Reagan, seriously. It was just a strange thing to say out of nowhere, that's all."

She doesn't look convinced, so I pick my plate up and shovel another bite of food into my mouth, all the while thinking about flamingo tongues in place of the ham on my sandwich.

When she smiles, God, it feels good. It's a weird thing to say about someone's smile. But when it's directed at me? Damn.

She finishes chewing the last of her sandwich, and I stand to take our plates to the kitchen. "Explain why you thought to bring up flamingo tongues while I make us a coffee. You have coffee in here, right?" I call over my shoulder as I go.

I hear her snort, and I grin. This chick.

"Of course I have coffee; I'm not a serial killer. There's a pod machine by the toaster and an array of pods to suit every mood in the stand beside it. Mugs are in the cabinet above," she calls back.

She's silent for a solid thirty seconds, probably trying to dodge my other question.

"Flamingo tongues, Reagan. Talk."

Her sigh is audible all the way from here, and I'm grinning like a fool again.

"Okay, so I'm not just some crazy who likes weird shit. It's literally what I do. It's my job. I'm the fact-checker at Pink Bits. I spend all day verifying random and quirky facts, and I freaking love it. But it leaves me a little ill-equipped when it comes to holding a normal conversation."

The job definitely suits her. But I have one question. I quickly make our coffees then stride back into the lounge carrying two steaming mugs of life-giving liquid. "What the fuck is Pink Bits? It sounds like a strip club, and I don't think the clientele go to those places for fun facts."

I sit on the edge of the seat she's on. In my rush to make the coffees, I hadn't noticed the mugs I'd pulled out for us to use… until now. Mine says, *The Muggle Struggle is Real,* and the one I grabbed for Reagan says, *She Believed She Could, So She Ate The Whole Pizza.*

"Nice cups," I say as I hand over hers. "Hope you like it with milk and sugar, 'cause I made it on autopilot and forgot to ask."

Her fingertips graze mine as she takes it from me, and I swear I feel a spark shoot up my arm. *I'm turning into Simon.* A shudder crawls under my skin, and I have to shake my arm out to get rid of the feeling.

Reagan quirks a brow. "You okay?"

I look at her like she's the crazy one here. "Uh, yeah. So back to your job. Pink Bits—strip joint?"

She takes a sip of her coffee and hums as she swallows. My dick twitches. I close my eyes and think of my grandma in her underwear. Only when I'm sure my dick has gotten the message do I lift her feet and slide back farther on the couch, then place them in my lap, down near my knees.

I take a swig from my cup to distract myself from her reaction to it, and damn, it's good.

With a flick of her tongue, she removes a drop of coffee from the corner of her lip, then answers my question. "No, Pink Bits is not a strip joint. It's my father's female hygienics company. You've never heard of the Pink Bits brand before?"

I shake my head. "I don't have any reason to know anything about female hygiene products, so that's a no for me. But now that you say it, the name fits. It's actually kinda cool."

She smiles proudly. "It really is. My dad has done wonderful things in the industry."

But I'm struggling to understand why a company that makes that kind of shit needs a fact-checker. "And where do you come into the equation? I'm not seeing it."

Shuffling back slightly, she lifts her hand to gesticulate as she speaks with way more excitement than I think the topic requires, but I love how into it she is. "Right. So, pads and tampons are nobody's idea of a good time. They're ugly and boring. So, I came up with the idea of putting random little facts on the packaging for women to read while they're doing the mandatory change over."

Her eyes are shining like sapphires; I can't look away. They sparkle as she speaks, and I'm caught in a daze as she blabs on about something I really don't care to know about. But her excitement makes me want to hear every word she has to say.

I am so utterly screwed.

Reagan

I'm doing it again—talking incessantly. But I'm so passionate about Pink Bits and my role in the company. "What woman wants to look at a bland sticky strip on the inside of her pad when she could be finding joy in the fact that you can create five new starfishes by cutting one single starfish into pieces? I mean, how cool is—" He's looking at me like he wants to kiss me, and I stumble over my words.

My train of thought has officially left the building.

Rhett's eyes fix on my face. He's listening so closely to every word I'm saying that I'm suddenly nervous. That never happens. My lack of filter is my weakness; I get the slightest bit nervy and I blurt inappropriate facts. But now I'm having trouble even finding my tongue.

A shiver I can't suppress runs from the tips of my toes up my leg, and I realise he's gently running his fingers over my tender foot. His gaze locks on mine. My skin prickles as his rough hand slides across my ankle and over my calf on its way up my body.

"Swans are the only birds with an external penis!" I blurt.

Oh my God.

Yes, ladies and gentlemen, I just said that out loud to my sexy-as-sin neighbour.

Kill me now.

Chapter Five

Rhett

I'M ABOUT TO TELL HER JUST HOW STUNNING HER eyes are when those words explode from her mouth. My hand freezes midway up her toned thigh. "What?"

She holds her breath for a moment before expelling it in a rush. "It's the most recent fact I entered into the database: swans are the only birds with an external penis. All other birds have internal ones that only come out to play when it's showtime."

A deep, rough laugh erupts from my belly. This chick is fucking crazy, and I'm loving every second of it. She's so random. I'm never sure what's going to come out of her mouth. I mean, I was in the process of making a move on her, but I'm not upset that she ruined the moment. Actually, I think she made it better.

When my laughter subsides, I can't help but smile at the blank expression on her gorgeous face. "What now? What's wrong?"

A deep crease forms between her perfectly shaped brows. "I thought for sure you would have been out the door by now, but you're still here."

"Yeah, and?"

The corner of her lip is trapped between her teeth as she gnaws on it. I can't stand seeing her like that, unsure of herself. I reach forward, slide my palm around her jaw and free her lip with my thumb. "Don't do that. I like your brand of crazy. You don't have to try and hide it from me."

Her grin is blinding. It lights up her entire face, widens her bright eyes, and takes my breath away.

With my hand still cupping her face, my thumb glides over her full, pouty bottom lip. "You have a beautiful mouth," I tell her. It's not a smooth compliment, but it's an honest one.

"Yeah?" she exhales.

I nod. "Fuck yeah."

I'm so close to her now I can feel her breath on my own lips, and I don't even recall moving up the couch. She has me under some kind of spell.

I want to kiss her.

I want to feel her skin under my palms.

I want to hear her breathy moans as I slide inside of her.

I want. I want. I want.

Suddenly, her eyes widen in pain, and her breath hitches. "My foot," she gasps.

I'd forgotten I was still nursing her injured foot in my hand, and my lust-driven thoughts must have caused my grip to tighten. Asshole!

Immediately, I release her, sliding back down the end of the couch to inspect the damage I've just inflicted. Blood has seeped through to the top of the fresh dressing. Shit.

I place my hand over the red smear to hide it from her. "It's all good down here. Sorry I hurt you; I didn't mean to. I was just looking at your lips and got carried away. I'm so fucking sorry, Reagan."

With a grimace, she tries to comfort me. "It's alright. It didn't hurt that bad ..."

I close my eyes against the obvious lie. "Reagan, it did. *I* did. Again." Seems like that's all I'm good at with this girl. Our first encounter and I've landed her in hospital, needing stitches, then squeezed the wound so tightly I made her bleed. I'm on a roll today.

"I should go and let you get some rest," I tell her, lifting her feet from my lap and gently depositing them back on the couch when I stand. My hand lingers on her ankle, though. I should cover the bloodied patch before I leave in case it sends her loopy when she spots it.

Holding up a finger, I instruct her to stay put, then retrieve one of the replacement dressings the doc gave us and place it directly on top of the current one.

Satisfied I've done a good thing, I know I need to leave before doing something else to cause her pain.

"I'll check in on you tomorrow?" I ask more than state as I turn to leave her.

Silence greets my back. Glancing over my shoulder, I see she's staring out the window. "Reagan?" I prompt. Her face is expressionless when she returns her gaze to me. I swallow. "I'll see you tomorrow?"

She nods her head once, then goes back to looking out the window.

Reagan

AND THERE YOU HAVE IT, FOLKS: HOW TO SCARE A man away in less than twenty-four hours.

I feel even more pathetic now than I did last night, coming home to my empty apartment on a Friday evening with no plans for the weekend.

It's not like we were off to a good start anyway—what with the glass in the foot and all. But we could have been friends; I would have liked that. I don't think he'll be back tomorrow. He's probably on the phone to the landlord now, abandoning his lease and searching for a new apartment building where he won't ever have to run into the awkward girl again.

I need Char's input on this. My eyes roam the room, searching for my phone, and I spot it on the TV cabinet. Roughly calculating the distance from my position on the couch to my goal, I figure I can make it no worries. It's like ten feet, max.

Swinging my legs around, I gingerly place them on the floor. I won't need the crutches for such a short jaunt. Licking my lips, I use my hands to push myself up and off the couch. I manage one, two, three steps—*shit!*

I cry out as I crumple in a heap in the middle of the room. My foot burns, and the stitches pull tight. I lie on the floor for a good five minutes, waiting for the pain to subside, before deciding to crawl the rest of the way to the TV cabinet. A wave of victory washes over me as my fingers curl around my phone.

"SUCCESS!" I yell as I slide back to the floor and crawl my way to the couch.

Once I'm comfortably situated with my feet propped up by some throw pillows, I call Char. It rings for so long I think her voicemail is going to pick up, but it's Char's breathy voice that greets me.

"Hiya," I chirp.

"Hey, s'up?" she croaks.

I'm on high alert instantly. "What's wrong? You sound like death."

"I wish I was dead. There is no pain in death."

Oh shit. With everything that happened this morning, I forgot she had an endo flare-up last night. "Still hurting, babe?"

I hear Char swallow. "Yeah, you could say that. Or you could say Freddy Krueger has taken up residence in my uterus."

Dear God. I've never been more thankful for the mild cramps I experience during shark week. "Sorry, honey. I'd offer to come lounge around with you, but I'm out of action. Long story short, my naked hot neighbour barged into my apartment this morning, I dropped my hammer and smashed the coffee table, and then stood on not one, but two massive shards of glass. He saw ALL my crazy when he took me to the hospital, but he stayed and took care of me even when I puked on him. He's so sweet." I sigh at the loss of what could have been—at the very least—a beautiful friendship.

"I'm sorry, what? Back right up, sugar tits, 'cause it sounded like you said the sexy piece of man meat who lives next door to you appeared inside your apartment naked this morning," Char says, completely ignoring everything I've said except the naked neighbour bit.

"Yes, Char, but you missed the rest of it. And I'm not even done yet."

"The rest doesn't matter unless it ended in hot, sweaty sex," she retorts.

"I wish!" I snort.

"Oh babe," Char coos. "What happened?"

"I think he was going to kiss me, but my mouth got in the way again. I told him swans have external penises." I groan at my stupidity.

Char bursts out laughing. "Damn, girl, that is priceless. What'd he do?"

"He laughed. Said he liked my crazy and that he thinks I have a beautiful mouth. Then, he accidently squeezed my ripped-up foot real hard, and he said he had to go." I'm still trying to work out exactly where I went wrong. It seemed like he liked me, like he wasn't put off by my quirks.

"Dude, he's totally into you," Char says.

I scoff. "Did you not just hear a word I said? This

disaster is my life, Char, and I'm tired of it. You should have seen it; it was brutal."

I just know she's rolling her eyes at me. "I didn't need to be there. From what you just told me, he's into you. Trust me, I know these things. My sexy-time senses are tingling. You're being dramatic."

My nose scrunches. I'm sceptical, at best, about Char's claim to have special sexual senses. "Your sexy-time senses can't pick up stuff that you're not even around to see unfold. That's not how those kinds of things work."

"Uh, yes they do. What would you know anyway? Your superpower is weirding people out with obscure facts. Mine is knowing when someone is attracted to another person."

It's my turn to roll my eyes. "They are not superpowers, Char. They're social handicaps, at best. You thought your gynaecologist was into you, but he was just doing his job. I think you're just as off the mark with this situation."

Char takes a sharp inhale of breath, and I know what it means: she's in a lot of pain.

"Babe, we can talk about this later. The doc gave me some good pain pills for my foot. I can try to figure out a way to get them to you if you need them," I offer. I hate not being able to help her when she's like this.

"Pfft, your pain pills have got nothing on mine." She breathes slow and deep. "I'll be fine. I was just trying to stretch out the time between doses. It was a stupid idea. I should have taken them a half hour ago. Now I have to wait for this lot to kick in."

"Okay," I mumble, feeling shitty about not being there for her right now. "I'll call you tomorrow to check on you."

"I know you will. And, Reagan, he's into you." She makes kissy sounds, then hangs up.

Lying on my couch, I stare at the ceiling and contemplate my best friend's words. Could he really be into me? Could Rhett be my unicorn?

It's with these thoughts running through my mind that I fall asleep.

Chapter Six

Rhett

I'm sweating like a pig. Lying completely starkers on my couch isn't even helping with this oppressive heat. What I really need to do is buy a whole new air conditioner, but that requires more effort than I'm willing to put in right now.

After the events of yesterday, I just want to spend the day doing sweet F.A. But this heat is too much; I'm dying in here.

I jerk upright when I remember I told Reagan I would check on her this morning. Scanning the room, I search for my long-forgotten pants. Spotting them over the back of one of my dining chairs, I snatch them up on my way past.

A minute later, I'm knocking on Reagan's front door.

First silence, then a faint "hello" reaches my ears,

and I call back, "It's me, Rhett. Checking on you, as promised."

I can hear her shuffling around inside, a few muted curses, and then the door swings open. She's in the same tank I gave her yesterday and those sexy little shorts. My eyes eat her up; she's a hot mess.

"Hey," she greets and hobbles out of the way on her crutches, allowing me entry.

Sliding in past her, I don't miss the way her eyes track over my bare chest. It feels good—her eyes on my body, taking me in. Makes me feel like less of a creeper when I check her out—which is a lot.

I'm almost past her when my foot catches on one of her crutches, and I go down like a tonne of bricks.

"Oh my God, I'm sorry! Are you okay?" she asks from above me, her blue eyes wide and searching.

"I'm good," I assure her, shuffling out from under her and bouncing back to my feet. I don't even care that I face-planted; the temperature in here feels like heaven on my overheated flesh. Smirking at the miserable look on her gorgeous face, I ask, "What's wrong? You in pain?"

She shakes her head. "No, but I tripped you up. Not only am I awkward, I'm a klutz too," she says with a shrug. "I'm just a little over it all today."

I lead the way into her lounge. "You need anything? Have you eaten this morning?"

"Nah, I only woke up not long ago. I've been dozing in and out on the couch. The pain meds make me sleepy."

Well, that gives me something useful to do while I soak up the cool air coating my sweat-slicked skin. "Alright, you sit, and I'll feed you," I tell her while moving towards her kitchen. She doesn't argue.

I open her fridge and pull out the eggs and bacon I saw in there yesterday, then check her drawers for a fry pan—bingo. It takes me ten minutes to whip up some fried eggs and bacon on toast for both of us since I haven't eaten either. And we can't forget the caffeine.

"Here you go, gorgeous," I say with a flourish as I pass her a plate and a steaming mug of coffee, then duck back into the kitchen to grab my own.

When I take the seat across from her, she looks up at me, eyes wide. "Wow, this looks great and smells amazing. I didn't even realise I was hungry."

I settle back in my seat and grin at her. "Can't go wrong with bacon."

She smiles back, then pops an extra crispy piece in her mouth. "Amen to that."

Just like yesterday, we eat in comfortable silence.

Until Reagan breaks it. "Did you know that coffee can be lethal in mass quantities?"

I quirk a brow and take a sip from my mug. This

one says, *Sexy, Sassy and a Little Badassy*. I snort at it before answering her. "No, that's news to me. And exactly how much coffee does one have to ingest for it to kill them?"

Her answering chuckle warms my insides as much as the coffee I'm drinking. "Planning a murder, are we?" she asks.

"If I told you, I'd have to kill you," I tell her, my expression deadpan.

She shrugs. "Ten grams, or one hundred cups, in a four-hour period will do the trick, just for future reference. It might come in handy one day."

"Good to know. Got any other stealthy murder techniques for me? Purely for curiosity's sake, of course."

Grinning, she tilts her chin then purses her lips. "Nutmeg is extremely poisonous if injected intravenously."

"No shit?" I muse.

Her eyes light up. "Oh, and just one shot of the teeny tiny blue-ringed octopus's venom can kill twenty-six adult humans within minutes."

"Seriously? That's unsettling." I cringe at the thought of such a small creature being so deadly. My skin crawls, and I have to shake my arms out to be rid of the sensation.

Reagan's throaty laugh fills my ears, and I fix my gaze on her. "What?"

"You," she says between chuckles. "Your reaction—it makes me think you'd be afraid of spiders."

My eyes narrow. "And so what if I am?"

She beams. "You are, aren't you?"

Gritting my teeth, I mutter, "I didn't say that."

"You didn't have to." She laughs, her cheeks and eyes bright with mirth.

I roll my eyes. "Whatever, it's not a big deal. I just don't like the creepy little fuckers. I'm not afraid of them or anything. I just avoid them if I can."

"Aha, I'm sure you're not afraid. Not a big manly man like yourself." She snickers.

Finishing my food, I take my empty plate and mug to the kitchen. "I'm glad I amuse you." I huff on my way past her. Rinsing off my dirty dish, I slide it into the little single-drawer dishwasher, then rummage through Reagan's coffee pods. "You want a refill?"

"What kind of question is that?" she calls back.

"A polite one. I could just make myself another, and you can watch me drink it?"

She laughs again. The sound is quickly becoming one of my new favourites.

"Okay, fine. Although, I don't see you making

such a dick move. Not when you've been so nice to me so far. I'll have a French vanilla latte please."

I poke my head around the corner to see her leaning over the back of the couch, facing the kitchen and me. "Don't doubt my ability to be a dick. I have skills you've never seen before."

Her grin is downright seductive. "I bet you do. I've seen enough to never doubt your particular skill set," she says with a waggle of her brows.

I burst out laughing and shake my head at her. "I think I'll keep you."

She stretches out her arm to me, her empty mug hanging from her fingers.

Closing the space, I snatch it from her. "You are somethin' else, Reagan."

"A good something or a bad something?" she asks my back as I return to the kitchen.

I consider her question. I've never come across a woman like her. She's a breath of fresh air. But I need to be careful; I can see myself becoming addicted to it. To her. Clearing my throat, I answer her as honestly as I can. "I'm not sure yet. I'll let you know."

Reagan

I SLEPT IN MY BED LAST NIGHT AND THOUGHT about Rhett on the other side of the wall that separates our apartments as I fell asleep. That's not creepy, right?

He stayed for most of the day yesterday. It was nice to have his company. We sat around watching movies and eating junk food. He even changed the dressing on my foot for me.

He'd said he would pop in before he left for work this morning, too, but I'm not sure when that will be. I'm kinda stressing about it. I like having him around, and I'm amazed I haven't scared him off yet.

I've been lying here, staring at the clock on my bedside table for the last twenty-three minutes, wondering what time he leaves for work. It's now six-fifteen, and I'm busting to pee. Should I hold it and go after he leaves or risk him coming while I'm peeing?

Stuff it, I'm about to pee my pants if I hold it any longer. Rolling off the side of my bed, I reach for my crutches and hobble to my adjoining bathroom. Leaning one crutch against the wall, I use my now free hand to roll my shorts and underwear down my legs.

My head drops back in pleasure as I pee, and pee, and pee some more. I think this is the longest pee I've ever done. And it feels so good.

And, of course, that's the moment Rhett arrives.

The sound of his knocking echoes through my apartment, and I try to hurry up the waterworks, but it's not happening. It just keeps coming. "Give me a minute!" I call and hope he hears me.

Finally, I'm down to a trickle, and I snatch up the toilet paper to wipe, then grasp for my shorts, but they've fallen off my feet. I'm left with my undies sitting around my ankles. Grabbing them, I yank them up my legs as fast as I can one-handed. I can hear Rhett calling me—he sounds concerned.

"I'm coming!" I yell out as I quickly wash and dry my hands. Hygiene first, always.

I'm puffed by the time I reach my front door and swing it open. "Morning," I murmur on a particularly harsh exhale.

Rhett is standing in front of me in a dirty, grease-stained pair of jeans and navy button-down that's also covered in smudges. My eyes roam over him, and a little drool pools in my mouth. Wow. His biceps strain against the sleeves of his shirt, reminding me of what's under it.

Holy sexy mechanic. A dreamy little sigh escapes as I stare at him while catching my breath.

He frowns. "Ah, Reagan, are you okay?"

My eyes snap up to meet his. "Yeah, why?"

One of his thick eyebrows arches at my question. "You're wearing a pair of Batman panties, I can see your nipples through your tank, and you're panting ..."

I swallow hard at his description. "I wasn't flicking my bean if that's what you're thinking."

Both his brows lift, and his eyes widen. "Flicking your bean?"

"Yeah, you know: polishing the pearl, auditioning finger puppets, jilling off. I swear my hands were not in my pants. See?" I hold my right hand up to his nose to prove that there are no suspicious smells coming from me.

"Oh my God, woman." He buckles over laughing.

His head is now level with my bits. He might be down there laughing, but the visual is giving me other ideas. And they are not friend-zone ideas.

Snap out of it, Reagan! You're such a perv. Or just really hard up? Shaking my head at myself, I shuffle around him then hobble down the hallway to the lounge and plonk on the couch with a huff.

"Hey, where are you going?" Rhett calls after me.

I'm staring up at my ceiling one minute. The next, Rhett's head is hovering above me. I cover my face with my hands.

"Hey," he coos. His calloused palms wrap around my wrists and pry my hands away from my face. "I told you, you don't need to hide your crazy from me."

I frown. "I wasn't— Wait, you think I was being crazy?" *Was I?* I was just trying to get my head straight. That was why I walked away. Well, hobbled away.

Rhett smiles. "Well, you just held your fingers up to my nose to prove you weren't masturbating. That's a little crazy, babe."

Huh, okay. "I was just proving my point." I shrug.

"So, if you weren't embarrassed, why'd you do a runner?" he asks, still hovering over the back of the couch, staring down at me.

My jaw drops open, then snaps shut again. Nope. Not going there. I avert my gaze, avoiding his probing stare.

"Reagan," he says smoothly, "look at me."

I don't, choosing to ignore his request, until his hands wrap around my cheeks and he moves his head to the side. Right into my line of sight. Sighing, I stop acting like a child, letting our eyes lock and hold. "You don't want to know, so just let it go. Please?"

His eyes search my face for an uncomfortable moment, then he nods. "Okay, I'll let it go this time. Coffee?"

Relief has my lips lifting into a smile. "Please and thank you."

Rhett clatters around in my kitchen, already knowing where everything is. It feels good having him in my space. He fits in here. I think we were always supposed to be friends, just like Char and me. He seems to get me, and he can read me way too well for someone who only recently entered my life.

I'm lost in my thoughts when the couch dips beside me, and the smell of freshly brewed coffee fills my nostrils. I could get used to this.

Rhett

A PART OF ME IS DYING TO KNOW WHAT SHE refuses to tell me. But another part knows she's keeping it to herself for good reason. I know already that there's not much she won't say, so I can respect her wanting to keep this to herself.

Slinging my arm over the back of the couch behind her feels natural. Sitting here with her, drinking my morning coffee—which tastes better than the shitty coffee in my apartment—feels right. I've never felt so comfortable in a woman's home before.

Before I'm ready, my phone alarm goes off, letting me know I need to leave for work. I'm fully booked at the garage, otherwise I would have considered taking the morning off to chill with Reagan.

"That's me. I gotta roll," I tell her.

The smile that has been gracing her face for the last half hour drops slightly. "Oh, okay. Thanks for checking in."

I take her empty mug from her. "I'll make you another before I go," I say, taking our cups into the kitchen. After placing mine in her dishwasher, I snap a pod into her machine and make her a fresh cup.

"Here you go, beautiful." With a grin, I hand her the mug that says *Chaos Coordinator*. "This cup was made for you." I grin. "You need anything before I go?"

Looking up at me, she purses her lips. "Umm, my laptop? It's on the kitchen bench."

"You got it." I retrieve her MacBook then, handing it to her, I press a kiss to the top of her head.

"I'll see you tomorrow," I say over my shoulder as I head for the door.

Closing it behind me, I pause—why did I just kiss her head? That's a boyfriend move, and I am not that kind of guy. I didn't even think about it; I just did it.

It's not a big deal though, right? I mean, it's not like I kissed her on the mouth or anything.

Yeah, no big deal. I nod to myself. Right, no big deal.

Maybe if I tell myself that enough, I'll start to believe it.

Chapter Seven

Reagan

I spend the day going through the most recent lot of fact proposals from the Pink Bits website submission tool. Sometimes I get some good ones that come in, but it's mostly just crap people have made up or old wives' tales. I have to confirm every single one before I can then enter it into the database.

Before I know it, it's five in the afternoon and I've spent the whole day on my couch with my laptop. I made myself a coffee and a sandwich at some point and hobbled to the toilet a couple of times. But other than that, I haven't moved.

My foot is aching, and I need to get up and take more pain meds before it gets too bad. I'm shifting around, about to get up, when my phone chimes for the first time today.

It's my daddy. I smile at his message.

DADDY: Hey Pumpkin, I'll drop in with some takeout on my way home in an hour. Feel like anything in particular? You better be resting when I get there.

ME: Dim Sum, pretty please. Love you, Daddy.

Looking down at myself, I decide I should put on some clothes before he gets here. We're super close, but even we have boundaries. I don't ever want to see him in his underwear, so I'll give him the same courtesy.

I gingerly place my feet on the floor and slowly lift myself to standing. Putting most of my weight on my good foot, I slip my crutches under my arms and head towards the kitchen. My pain pills are sitting on the counter, and I pop two with a glass of water, then make my way to my bedroom.

Once I get there, I collapse on my bed. "Jesus," I pant. That was a mission. When I've caught my breath, I sit up. Pants. I need to find pants. And then I catch a whiff of myself. "Oh God." I gag. I realise I haven't had a shower in two days.

Yuck, yuck, yuck!

Shower. I need a shower. Wriggling until I'm at the edge of my bed, I get to my feet again. This time, I move towards my adjoining bathroom without my crutches. I make it two steps, then falter when I have to put weight on my bad foot. *Shit.*

Clutching the doorframe, I take a breath then hop into the room, each bounce making my boobs just about slap me in the face and my foot throb. Plonking down on the toilet, I realise I won't be able to get in the shower because I can't get my foot wet. The dressing isn't waterproof, and I probably wouldn't be able to stand under the spray unassisted anyway.

"Ugh," I groan in frustration. There is no freaking way I'm staying like this, though. So I slide to the floor, open the small cupboard door under my sink and grab a cloth, the extra bottle of body wash I have stashed away in there, and some feminine wipes.

Twenty gruelling minutes later, I'm as clean as I'm going to get without hopping in the actual shower. And I'm exhausted. Dear God, am I exhausted. You don't realise how much you use one bloody limb until you can't.

I grab the first pair of shorts I can find and slide them up my legs. And I do alright until I get to my arse, since I'm still on the floor. I'm wriggling around, hoisting my pants over my bubble butt, when I hear my front door swing open.

"Pumpkin, you in here?" my dad's voice echoes down the short hallway.

"Coming!" I call back, then roll onto my tummy and up to my knees. Snatching my crutches up, I hook them under my arms and trudge out to my lounge. "Hey, Daddy," I greet him and smile wide at the site of the big-arse bag of food he's bought me.

He sends me a nod as he makes his way to my kitchen. "Where's your coffee table?" he asks.

I can hear him pulling out plates and cutlery when I take my spot on the couch. "Umm, I broke it."

"You broke it? How?" he asks, coming in to sit by me with two plates full of little buns and dumplings that smell incredible.

"Ah, well, if you must know, I dropped a hammer on it. I was thinking of changing things up in here anyway, so no biggy." I shrug.

He nods along before saying, "I see. And I'm assuming this is how you hurt yourself then? When you rang and said you wouldn't be coming to work this week because you'd hurt your foot, I thought maybe you'd tripped in those ridiculous high heels you insist on wearing and sprained it, or something like that."

I'd called HR on Monday morning to let them know I wouldn't be coming in and gave them very little explanation. I'm the boss's daughter; nobody questions me. Then I was super vague about it all when I spoke to Dad on Saturday night. I chose to avoid having the detailed conversation over the phone. He would have freaked and no doubt overreacted. I let him think what he wanted.

I shove a little ball of pork-and-chive heaven in my mouth and nod. "Uh-huh," I mumble through my mouthful of food.

Dad gives me the side-eye. "You going to tell me what happened?"

I finish chewing, then swallow. "You going to tell me why you're eating dinner with me and not Cruella de Vil this evening?"

He snorts. "Nice deflection. How about, I'll tell if you do?"

Popping another dumpling in my mouth, I consider his offer. I chew slowly, assessing my father; he looks tired. The light that normally emanates from his steely blue eyes isn't there today. I don't like it. Narrowing my own, I finally say, "You go first."

With a tilt of his head, he concedes. "Okay, Susanna and I aren't getting along that well right now. I can't handle another conversation about flower arrangements for her daughter's wedding—that I'm paying for, mind you. Why is that, you ask? I asked it myself, and you know what she told me? She said it's because Marianna is as much my daughter as she is hers. Can you believe that shit? When I corrected her, she slapped me." He shakes his head. "Susanna's ex-husband makes more money than I do. So why isn't he paying for *his* daughter's goddamn wedding?"

I blink, and blink again. I was not expecting all that. My father's face is getting redder by the second, and I have zero clue what to say to him. I don't particularly like my stepsister, but I don't not like her either. I don't really know her. We were grown when our parents married, so it's not like we're a real family in that sense. I sure as hell don't think he should be paying for her wedding, but I don't think now is the time to agree with him. I need to calm him down, not rile him up more.

"So, Marianna is getting married?" That's the best I can come up with.

Dad sighs. "Apparently."

"Did she ask you to pay for it?" I wonder aloud.

"No. She's been at the house a lot, organising it with her mother, but I try to avoid them when they're in wedding mode." He sighs again, lifting one hand to cup his forehead and rub his temples with his pointer and thumb. "It's not that I don't like the girl. She's perfectly fine. And the money's not the issue either. It's just that I don't think it's my place to be paying for her wedding. Not when her own father is

PINK BITS

in a position to do it. I'd lose my shit if another man tried paying for yours," he says, looking directly into my eyes.

"Aww, thanks, Daddy. But don't hold your breath on that one. I may as well spray myself with man repellent for all the luck I have. Maybe you should just embrace this; it might be your only chance."

His eyes darken at my statement. "Don't start that shit with me again, Reagan. There is nothing wrong with you. You're fucking perfect. You hear me?"

My eyes prickle. He's always been my biggest supporter in everything that I do and especially in everything that I am. "Okay," I breathe, then straighten my spine. "There actually is someone I might be a little interested in. But I'm not sure. I think we'll just end up friends. And I'm okay with that, too."

The light that has been missing in his eyes since he arrived sparks to life. "Go on, who is he?"

I grin. "My neighbour, Rhett Jones. Don't get carried away, though. We only officially met over the weekend. He was here when I cut myself." I gesture down to the white dressing that covers half my foot. "He took real good care of me: drove me to the hospital, and even stayed when Psycho Reagan emerged."

"He stayed?" he asks, his shock reflected in his tone. "He sounds like a keeper to me. If he can handle you when you're like *that*"—he cringes—"then he must be a good guy."

Rolling my eyes, I shove him. "Gee, thanks, Daddy."

Wrapping his arm around my shoulder, he pulls me into his side. "I'm glad he was here for you when you needed someone. I really do worry about you being alone so much, pumpkin." He squeezes me gently. "I promise not to get my hopes up if you promise to at least give this a try. Don't settle for friendship if you feel more for him."

I swallow hard, then nod. "Okay."

Chapter Eight

Rhett

My fist raps against Reagan's front door all of three times before it swings open. A fresh-faced Reagan stands before me in a way-too-small Superman tee that—if I'm not mistaken—has a little cape attached to the back. My grin is instant.

"Morning, beautiful," I greet her.

She beams up at me. "Morning. I got up extra early to pee so you wouldn't catch me off guard again."

"You didn't have to do that. I don't mind waiting out here for you to do your girly shit."

She rolls her eyes. "That would just be rude. Besides, yesterday you clearly thought I'd been having some *me time*, and I didn't want you to think that again." She shrugs. "Anyway, I was awake. I just didn't lie there like a lush for the extra half hour like I did yesterday."

I reach out and scruff her hair up as I slide past her, then stride down the hallway. "Whatever. I prefer my version of events over yours." I continue through the lounge area to her kitchen and get to making our coffees and breakfast.

Instead of waiting for me on the couch, she hobbles in after me, sliding onto a high bar stool on the other side of the bench and resting her crutches beside her. She watches as I go straight to the cabinet that holds her mugs and examine them all before picking two for today.

"You like my collection?" she asks.

Looking over my shoulder, I grin at her. "It's impressive."

Her smile comes out and brightens the whole room. "Which ones did you decide on?"

I hold them up to show her. The one I got out for myself has a picture of a great white shark and says, *What doesn't kill you makes you stronger ... except sharks. Sharks will kill you.* And the one I chose for her has a little Yoda on it and the words, *Coffee I need or kill you I will.*

She grins at my choices. "Did you know you're more likely to be attacked by a cow than a shark?"

Her eyes sparkle as she speaks, and I fucking love

how into all these random facts she is. "I did not know that. But I believe it, mostly because you couldn't pay me to set foot in the ocean. So that eliminates shark attacks completely for me."

Silence hits my back, and I turn around slowly to see why she's gone quiet. Her hand is covering her mouth, and I lean back against the bench behind me, then cross my arms and ankles. "What now?"

"Is it because you're afraid of the teeny tiny blue-ringed octopus?" She snorts, trying to hold back her laughter.

I roll my eyes. "No, it's all the other fucking huge shit in there that can—and would most definitely—eat me. I'm fucking delicious, don't you know?"

She erupts with laughter. Tears stream down her flushed cheeks as she attempts to calm herself and catch her breath, only for another round to take her under again. Then, I watch in slow motion as she tilts to the side and falls off her stool.

"Reagan!" I'm crouched at her side instantly. She's still laughing but rubbing her butt, too.

"I'm good!" she says quickly. "My arse took the brunt of it. Lucky I've got extra padding." She winks as I help her back up and onto the stool again.

"Jesus, woman, you need a crash helmet or something," I tell her, shaking my head and going back around the bench to start cooking our food.

What I don't say is how sexy I think that extra padding is. Instead, I nudge her coffee over and eye her. "Try not to burn yourself."

"Funny," she mumbles and flips me the bird.

When I finish making our omelettes, I slide into the seat next to her. "*Bon appetit.*"

"You're quite the chef, aren't you? I wish we'd met a long time ago; I could have been using you for your culinary skills all this time." She sighs dramatically.

I shove a forkful of the cheesy eggs into my mouth, then watch her do the same, grinning at me as she chews.

"Sho goog," she says through a mouthful.

Shaking my head, I turn my attention to my plate and shovel in some more before I accidentally tell her just how cute I think she is.

My plate is empty before hers—not surprising, seeing as I fixated on my food to keep myself from doing or saying anything stupid. After rinsing off my plate, I drop it into the dishwasher along with a couple of cups and plates she has sitting on the side of the sink.

"You don't have to do that," she says, her eyes following my every movement.

"I don't mind. Keeps my hands busy."

She cocks her head to the side. Her loose hair

falls over her shoulder, forming a blonde curtain. "Why do you need to keep your hands busy?"

Her plate is now empty, and I grab it, rinse it, and then place it in the dishwasher, too. "Dishwasher tablets?" I ask, glancing at her over my shoulder.

She licks her gorgeous lips, then points to the cupboard under the sink. "In there," she breathes and bites down on that full bottom lip.

Fuck me. *Is she trying to seduce me?* Because it's totally working. I want to walk over there, wrap my fingers in that mass of blonde, and tug her head back until she's staring up at me with those incredible eyes, then kiss the shit out of her.

I swallow hard and push my thoughts away. It's with superhuman strength that I keep myself in line and turn her dishwasher on. Leaning against the bench beside it, I slip my hands into my pockets. "Need me to change your dressing?"

She blinks a couple of times, then shifts her gaze to her foot. "Umm, yeah, if that's okay? You don't have to; I can ask—"

I hold my hand up, stopping her. "I'll do it. I don't mind." I smile reassuringly as I open another cabinet and retrieve the extra dressings the hospital gave her. I really just want to be able to touch her in a non-creepy way.

My attraction to her has grown exponentially

over the last couple of days, and it's unnerving. What if I banged her and she wanted it to keep happening? That's not my thing. We live next door to each other; it would get awkward as fuck. I don't want that for us. So, I need to keep it in my pants and keep her as my friend.

The word *friend* feels strange—a chick as a friend. It's a foreign concept to me, but I'm willing to give it a shot. I like Reagan way too much to fuck things up between us.

Reagan

Rhett is an amazing cook. He made an omelette taste like a gourmet meal.

I can't stop smiling at him, even though he's currently changing the nasty dressing on my foot. Keeping my focus on him ensures that I don't look at my foot and risk seeing blood. Just thinking about what he's doing—touching that area voluntarily—makes me a little swoony. Not in a bad way, but in a "he's so amazing to be doing this for me" kind of way.

"There you go. All done. And you'll be pleased

to know the skin has started knitting together, so you don't need to worry about seeing blood anymore."

I blink at him. "That was quick. Thank you."

He shrugs his wide, sculpted shoulders. "No problem. It's what I'm here for." He winks at me, and I swoon again.

This is ridiculous. I'm a puddle of goo and all he did was cook for me, make me coffee, and change my dressing. *Actually... having mushy feelings for him after doing all that is only natural, right?*

"You okay? There wasn't any blood; you shouldn't be feeling woozy ..." he says. The look in his eyes conveys his worry.

I shake my head in an attempt to clear it. "Yeah, no, I'm fine. I was just thinking, is all."

He raises a brow. "About what? You looked all spaced out."

My lips purse. Usually I have no issues sharing what's on my mind, but I think I'll freak him out if I tell him I'm having seriously swoony thoughts about him. I clear my throat. "Oh, you know, just normal stuff." I shrug. "I think I might be due to get my period in the next couple of days. I'm feeling hormonal."

His eyes widen. "Right, okay then. On that note, I've gotta be going." He glances at his watch. "I'll be late if I don't get on the road pretty soon."

At least I threw him off from my actual thought process. "Okay, thanks for checking in. And feeding me, and the coffee, and company."

A lopsided grin tilts his lips, and I internally swoon again. He's so freaking sexy. And he's not even trying to be, which makes him even sexier.

"You are very welcome, Reagan. I'll see you tomorrow," he says as he stands. Then, he bends down and presses his lips to my forehead and walks away.

I sigh, watching his behind as he strolls out of my apartment.

He is beyond sexy. And that arse? I want to bite it. I'm an arse girl, always have been. And his is amazing.

I hear Rhett knocking and, unlike yesterday, I'm not waiting at the door for him to arrive. I'm still hobbling down the hallway on his tenth knock. "I'm coming. I'm coming!" I yell loud enough for him to hear me through the door.

Leaning on my now much prettier crutches, I swing the door open.

"Mornin', gorgeous," Rhett drawls, propped against the door frame.

I smile up at him. I love how much taller he is than me. "Morning. Like the modifications I made to my ugly crutches?" I ask, tilting them back and forth so he can get the whole effect of the pretty sparkles glinting in the light.

His eyes move down my body, inch by inch, then they slide over to my crutches. "What the fuck?" he asks, a frown forming between his brows.

I grin. "I was bored last night. So, I bedazzled them!"

"I see," he says softly.

"Do you like them? I mean, I know they're still butt-ugly, but they look better, right?"

I can't describe the look on his face. It's not pained. Maybe it's indifferent? I'm not sure.

"Well, I don't *not* like them," he finally says.

Meh, I don't really care if he likes them or not. I think they look way better, and that's all that matters. I shrug, shuffle out of his way, and let him pass me.

"What I do like are those PJs," he says as he squeezes past me.

I look down and see the lightning bolt stretched across my chest. "Me too. You like The Flash?"

"I'm more of a Batman guy myself, but I can see the appeal of being Flash fast on occasion. I have always wondered, though, is he able to pace himself at times? Like when he gets excited?" He pauses and turns to eye me. "You know what I'm sayin'? Does he, like, lose control and fuck Flash fast? 'Cause that would suck."

In all honesty, it's something I've contemplated myself. "I've thought about that, too. I would hope not, but who can say?" I shrug. "Makes no difference to me; he's not my type."

Rhett tilts his chin. "He's not?"

I shake my head. "No. Speed isn't an attribute I'm looking for in a potential bedmate." I laugh at his perplexed expression.

His Adam's apple bobs as he swallows. "So, what are you looking for?"

That's a great question—one I'm not sure how to answer. My lips pinch as I consider it. What am I looking for? *Him!* my sex-deprived brain screams. Then my daddy's words echo in my head: *"Don't settle for friendship if you feel more for him."*

I'm ninety-nine percent sure I want more from him. So, I mentally pull up my big girl panties and tell him the truth. "Well, if I'm being honest, you're my type. Physically, for sure. And from the little I know of you, you tick all the boxes in the personality department, too."

I watch him carefully. He doesn't say anything, and I worry I've overstepped. "I'm sorry, I didn't mean—"

"No, it's fine. I'm a sexy beast. I know it, and you have eyes, so you know it, too." He winks.

"Umm, okay. Well, that right there." I point at his mouth. "What just came out of there—not an attractive quality in any man. Even one as sexy as you."

He grins. "Noted. Now, I need caffeine."

And that's the end of the conversation.

He strides into the kitchen and is pulling things out of the fridge by the time I make it to the counter and take my seat to watch him weave his culinary magic. I could watch him move around my kitchen all day long. A grin tugs at my lips as I imagine him doing just that—but naked.

It's Thursday, and I've adjusted to this little routine Rhett and I have going. I wake up at six, pee, and then make my way to my front door right in time for him to start knocking. I swing it open the second his knuckles connect with the wood.

He's leaning on the actual door this morning and tips forward, losing his balance. He tries to grab at the doorframe to stop us from colliding, but it's no use. His heavy body falls into mine, and I topple backwards. Rhett curls his arms around me, one at my waist, one behind my head, and we hit the ground with a thud.

All the air leaves my lungs in a rush. I swallow and try desperately to take a breath, but it doesn't work. He's still pressed flat against my chest, making inhalation impossible. My eyes widen as I struggle, and I start slapping at his back to get him to move.

"Fuck, Reagan. I'm sorry," he rambles, pushing his upper body up with his arms braced on either side of my head.

Relieved, I relish the air rushing back into my oxygen-deprived lungs. He's staring down at me now, and I can only imagine what's going through his mind. His eyes hint to a million different thoughts—all of them tantalising. But he just stays there, frozen.

Slowly lifting my hand, I press it to his jaw. My fingers feather over his stubbled cheek, and he closes his eyes. When my thumb grazes his bottom lip, they flash open again—the heat in them just about burns me alive. I want him to kiss me so, so badly. "Rhett," I sigh his name, and he leans into my touch.

His hot breath skitters along my wrist, sending tingles up my arm. Our eyes remain connected as he lowers his head, closing the gap between our mouths. He pauses a whisper away from my aching lips. "Reagan," he groans my name, then finally his mouth crashes into mine.

PINK BITS

The feel of his lips is intoxicating... and right. So, so right. But it's not enough. I need more, but he pulls his head back when I try to deepen the kiss.

"I don't do girlfriends. I don't date. I don't hang out. That's just not me, Reagan. But I want you so much," he confesses.

My stupid emotions rise to the surface. I am not a fuck-buddy kind of girl. It's just not who I am. But that's all he wants. I can see he's holding back; there's something he's not saying. He knows I want all the things he doesn't. My eyes sting, and I squeeze them shut. I don't want him to see that his words have hurt me.

He's been so amazingly sweet to me, and there's no reason we can't be friends. Keeping my eyes closed, I push my palms against his chest, letting him know I want him to move. He does so immediately, then takes one of my hands in his and helps me stand.

I lean against the wall as he scoops up my crutches and slides them under my arms. I'm thankful when he turns away from me, closes the door that's still wide open, and then makes his way down the short hallway.

But he pauses at the end. Keeping his back to me, he says, "You are the coolest chick I've ever met. If anyone could make me want to change my ways,

Reagan, it's you. Maybe one day, but I'm not there yet, and I refuse to give you less than you deserve."

Then he's gone.

Dropping my head back, I stare up at the ceiling. Of course I would find an amazing, sexy, funny, and sweet guy who can handle me at my worst, but he doesn't want me the way I want him. I take a few minutes to collect myself. *He didn't say never, right?* And we haven't known each other long. Maybe I just need to let things unfold on their own.

Nodding to myself, I push off the wall and go to find him.

I find him in the kitchen with two mugs of coffee already made and a perplexed expression on his handsome face as he leans back against the bench. His hands are shoved in his pockets, and his ankles are crossed.

He lifts his head when I enter. "I'm sorry," he murmurs. His eyes lock with mine.

I shake my head. "Don't be. You were honest with me. I can't fault you for that."

He snakes one big hand up around the back of his neck, rubbing it. "Yeah, but I just ..." He sighs and looks back down to his boots.

"Hey, it's all good. I promise. I know where you stand, and that's okay. As long as you know where I stand, too," I tell him.

His eyes lift to mine. "Where exactly do you stand? Just so there's no confusion going forward for either of us."

My lips lift in a shy smile, and I shrug. "I like you. I'm comfortable around you, and I don't feel so awkward and out of place when I'm with you. So, yeah, I would like to see if there's more there. But I'm not going to push you for something you're not willing to give. I'm fine with friendship if that's all you want."

Rhett watches me closely as I speak, nodding along. "Friendship is good. I've never really been friends with a chick, but I'd really like to try with you. I mean, we're friends already, aren't we?"

I can't contain my grin. "Yeah, I think so."

"Okay, good." A relieved smile tugs at his lips. "Now that that's out of the way, let's get some food into you."

Pulling out the stool I sat on yesterday, I hop onto it and rest my chin in my hand as I watch Rhett buzz around my kitchen, smiling to myself.

"What's that look about?" he asks over his shoulder, not stopping what he's doing.

"Just because you don't want me doesn't mean I can't still admire the view," I tell him, grinning when he drops the spatula he was holding.

Spinning around, he glares at me. "So this is how

it's going to be, is it? You can check out the goods, but I can't?"

I roll my eyes. "Pfft, like you can keep your eyes to yourself, you perv. You couldn't help yourself if you tried—you're staring at my tits right now."

His eyes bounce back up to mine. "You're not wearing a bra! And what the fuck are you wearing? Are they Powerpuff Girls?"

Grinning, I nod. "Yeah, they are! Powerpuff Girls are awesome. And you know how I feel about bras. This isn't a new development. I'm not going to start wearing one now just because you don't have any self-control."

He sighs and presses a hand to his heart. "Thank God. I was worried you'd start dressing like a nun."

I laugh. "Yeah, no. That's not going to happen... ever."

"Good." He smirks and turns back to the stove, preparing our breakfast.

Chapter Nine

Rhett

I've been thinking about her all day. So much so that I almost stuffed up an oil change. And you have to be pretty fucking stupid to stuff that up. I've never been interested enough in a chick to care what she was doing through the day. Now, I'm kicking myself for not getting Reagan's number so I could text her to check in.

I almost went back home on my lunch break just to check up on her—almost. How fucking pathetic is that? What? I can't go a full day without seeing her? I can't be pussy whipped. To be that, we'd have to have had sex. And we haven't.

It feels like I've known her a hell of a lot longer than a couple of days. Besides my sister, she's the first chick I've actually spent time around. And the thought of spending more time with her makes my heart beat faster with anticipation.

What the fuck is wrong with me? I'm turning into Simon. That pansy-arse bastard; he's gone and rubbed his lovesick-puppy shit all over me.

I scowl at my reflection in the steam-fogged mirror. *Snap out of it, dickhead. She's your friend.*

Drying myself off, my thoughts inevitably wander back to her and her reaction to my dick the day we met. My lips tug up in a smile. God, she is something else. And there I go again, thinking of her all fondly and shit.

I wasn't lying this morning when I told her if anyone could make me want to try for more, it would be her. She's smart, funny as shit, and so fucking sexy in that nerdy way that makes her not just sexy, but adorable, too. I've got half a chub just thinking about her.

Closing my eyes, I can almost smell the floral scent that coats her soft skin. I inhale deeply; I want her. And it's not just because she's hot. I knew she was before we actually met. We'd passed each other in the hallways before and shared the elevator a few times. I didn't start wanting her until I started getting to know her.

She's gotten under my skin in just a few short

days, and I don't know if I want to shake her off or tie myself to her.

Scrubbing my hand through my hair, I glare at myself again. I've never been so confused. I throw my towel on the rack to dry and stalk into my bedroom. After collapsing on the bed, I lie there, thinking about her on the other side of the wall until I fall asleep.

I'M NOT A MORNING PERSON. SO THE FACT THAT I've gotten out of bed the second my alarm has sounded every morning this week says a lot. Especially since it's set an hour earlier than usual so I can spend time with Reagan—I mean, check in on her.

I snort at myself. I think it's time to admit I'm not doing this for her benefit but my own. She puts me in a good mood for the rest of the day. I haven't thrown a spanner at my worker, Jake, all week.

Leaning over the small sink in my bathroom, I fill my hands with warm water and scrub at my face, then reach for my toothbrush and paste. I give my teeth a good once-over, then go into my spare room to rummage through my clothes. Finding a set of work gear, I throw them on, then slip my feet into my boots before walking out the door.

At six a.m. on the dot, I'm knocking at Reagan's door.

She opens it slowly, cautiously poking her head around, before opening it fully for me.

I frown down at her. "What's wrong?"

"Nothing, was just making sure we didn't have a repeat of yesterday. You know, when you fell through the door and nearly killed me." She smiles at me.

I have to force my hands to stay at my sides. That damn smile—it gets me every time. Clearing my throat, I push past her. "That's not exactly how I remember it. It was more like you couldn't wait to see me and threw the door open, knowing I would fall right into you. It was all a ploy for your dirty little hands to rub up on me."

She scoffs as she closes the door and hobbles along after me. "I don't think so. You're the one who can't keep your eyes off my tits. I think you positioned yourself just right so that you would fall into me, thereby giving you the perfect excuse to cop a feel."

I throw back my head, laughing as I open her fridge. "Yeah, okay, whatever you need to tell yourself. Now, let's see what we have to work with today." I scan the contents of her fridge and frown.

PINK BITS

She needs groceries. "You need to go shopping; your stocks are seriously depleted."

"That's your fault. You eat like a horse," she says from her spot on the bar stool.

True. I should probably get her some stuff to replace what I've eaten. "I'll take you tomorrow and go you halves."

"Okay."

"You've still got cheese and bread; how do you feel about grilled cheese for breakfast?"

"I'm good with whatever you put in my mouth," she chirps.

I straighten and stare at her. Does she even realise what she just said? One of my brows raises. "Whatever I put in your mouth? You're so dirty!"

She rolls her eyes. "*You* have a dirty mind. You know what I meant."

"I'm beginning to think you do this shit on purpose," I tell her, and the look of mock innocence that blankets her face gives her away. "You're such a bad liar."

Unable to contain her laughter any longer, she erupts. "Yeah, okay. You got me. But I don't mean things to sound that way when I say them. I usually only realise it after the words have left my mouth." She shrugs. "I don't really care though; I crack myself up."

"I bet you do." I shake my head at her, turn back to the kitchen, and start making our breakfast.

"How'd you get to be so comfortable in all your naked glory?"

I stop buttering the bread and look at her over my shoulder. "I don't know. I've just never been a shy kind of guy. Where the hell did that question come from anyway?"

"I was just staring at your butt, and Saturday morning popped into my mind. I'm kicking myself for not paying attention to it when you weren't wearing any pants." She sighs, her regret evident.

I swallow, my mouth suddenly feeling way too dry. I snatch a glass out of the cabinet, fill it with water, and down it. She's being her playful self. Nothing has changed between us, and I'm both relieved by the fact and a little frustrated. I mean, I don't want her to change, but it's her chill, "anything goes" personality that I'm attracted to. She's not making this easy on me.

Snapping myself out of my thoughts, I reply, "Right, well you had your chance. It was a one-time show. Not my fault you were so preoccupied with my cock you forgot to check out the buns, too."

A devilish grin spreads across her mouth. "It was hard to look past." She shrugs. "What can I say? It was just right there, you know? And it's very impressive. I was a little afraid of it for a minute, but something that perfect can't be scary. I wish you'd tell me his name. I don't like thinking of him as an inanimate object."

Stupid me for thinking this conversation couldn't get worse. She thinks about my dick. And damn, if that doesn't make him happy. He's paying attention now, listening to every word out of her devious little mouth.

"I'll tell you his name, if you tell me *her* name. Fair is fair." I dip my head down and gesture to her promised land with my chin.

She shrugs. "Okay. Her name is Mary."

My brows pucker in a deep frown. "As in, the Virgin Mary?"

"Ugh, no," she says, shaking her head adamantly. "As in, Mary, Queen of Scots."

"I don't get it."

She clenches her jaw, puckers her lips, and averts her eyes.

"Reagan, what aren't you telling me?" I prod.

A guttural groan fills the space, and I laugh at her dramatics.

"Fine! I'll tell you. Okay, so my first was a guy named Scot. It was super awful and awkward—as is every important moment in my life. Anyway, prior to this exchange with Scot, her name was Mary. Just

Mary. Afterwards, she became Mary, Queen of Scots. Then, as it happens, the next two men I slept with were also named Scott."

"Seriously? Was that by design? Or ... " I'm really fucking curious now.

Leaning her elbows on the bench, she rests her chin in her hands. "Not really. Not *my* design, anyway. But Char thought it would be hilarious, and seeing as she's like my only friend, she made it her mission to set me up with guys called Scot after I told her about Mary's name evolution."

I'm laughing so hard I have to support myself against the bench. "That is fantastic. I think I need to meet this friend of yours."

Lifting both her shoulders, her face remains expressionless. "She's just as strange as me. No, actually, she's worse. Much worse. Just so you know."

I grin. "She sounds like a good time."

She grumbles something to herself, then suddenly perks up. "Your turn!"

"Alright, alright." I take a deep breath. "Prepare yourself. It's pretty epic."

Her eyes glitter, and she shuffles to the edge of her stool, leaning farther forward on her elbows. "I'm ready. Tell me."

"His name is Prince Everhard of the Netherlands," I announce proudly.

It takes a solid five seconds for her to react. She blinks once, then twice, then her forehead hits the counter, and her whole body quakes with laughter.

My chest deflates. "It's a good name, dammit. I don't know why you're laughing."

I get no response this time. She completely ignores me as she gasps for air through her fits of laughter. I roll my eyes, then move about the kitchen, making our coffees.

Ten minutes later, she's wiping tears from her cheeks and grinning at me like the fucking Cheshire Cat. I glare back as I slide her mug of steaming coffee over to her. "I picked this mug just for you."

The cup I gave her has a picture of a cartoon uterus holding up a sign that reads, *Stay Nasty*. How fitting for the little creature sitting across from me.

She just shrugs and takes a sip of coffee. Dried tear streaks stick to her pink cheeks, and her eyes shine the brightest blue I've seen them yet. Why does she always have to look so damn appealing? It's frustrating as fuck. I run a hand through my hair, then snatch up the plates with our grilled cheese on them. "You're a killjoy, you know that?"

Her lips tug to the side. "Prince Everhard," she snorts, then composes her features by taking a deep breath. "That's the best name for a penis I've ever heard. Seriously, you were right, and I wasn't prepared."

I nod, satisfied. "Damn right it is."

Just as I'm about to leave for work, I remember to ask for Reagan's number. I enter her name as Queen of Scots in my phone, then put mine in hers as Prince Everhard.

Chapter Ten

Reagan

It's been exactly one week since I had a real shower. The thought makes me cringe. I showered before bed last Friday night, and that was the last time. I can't begin to express how much that disturbs me. I think I should be able to handle one now since my foot is feeling a little better.

I strip off my clothes and hobble into my bathroom. Leaning in, I reach for the tap when the distinct sound of knocking reaches my ears. I drop my head back. *You have got to be kidding me.*

Twisting around, I wobble my way back out, pausing to snatch my silky bathrobe off the back of my bedroom door. I wrangle it into place while balancing precariously on my crutches.

The knocking continues.

"I'm coming!" I yell down the hall, frustrated by

whoever is standing between me and my first shower in seven days.

When I reach the door, I tug it open with more force than necessary, causing the flimsy knot I tied in my robe to unravel with my jerky movements. Before I can do anything about it, Rhett's big hands are tugging the two sides back together for me.

"Holy shit," he breathes.

I watch his Adam's apple bob as he swallows hard. Then, keeping one hand curled tightly around the two sides of my robe, he reaches blindly for the ties with his free hand. Once he has both pieces, he ties them together so tight I know it's going to take me forever to untie them.

Only when he's satisfied that I'm fully covered does he speak. "Jesus, Reagan, what the hell? You can't answer your door like that. What if I was an axe murderer looking for my next victim?"

My eyes narrow on him. "If you were an axe murderer, I'd take you down with a swift crutch to the crotch," I shoot back. "And I didn't mean to answer the door like that. My robe was tied; it just came undone when I pulled the door open. I wasn't expecting anyone, and I was about to take a shower."

"A crutch to the crotch, huh?" He smiles.

I nod. "Yes. I may be incapacitated right now, but I still know how to protect myself."

PINK BITS

One of his hands rises to the back of his neck, rubbing it as he looks down at me. "Okay, well, sorry for interrupting you. I just... ah... I was just wondering if you wanted to eat with me tonight? We could get takeout?" He's looking at his boots when he says, "It's cool if you're sick of me, though."

My grin is instant. "I'd like that."

His eyes rise, meeting mine. "Great, good."

I shift to let him in, then close the door behind him. I follow him back to the lounge but hover by the hallway to my room. "I'm just going to shower. I'm dying to feel the hot water against my skin. It's been too long. You go ahead and order whatever, and I'll be out in a bit."

He nods. "Okay, cool."

My shower is the best. I have a sunken bath with the most amazing shower head above. I turn the water on, then slip my robe off. Leaning my crutches against the sink, I hold onto the wall and stare into the tub.

How the hell am I going to get down there?

Using the wall to keep my balance, I slide down until I'm on my butt, then slip my legs into the tub. Putting most of my weight on my good foot, I edge towards the hot spray of the water, sighing when it hits my body.

It feels incredible. I stand, absorbing the warmth

and letting the showerhead work its magic on my sore muscles. Getting around on crutches all week has got me aching in places I hadn't expected.

Tipping my head back, I close my eyes and let the water run over my face and down my body. My hair feels so nasty after using nothing but dry-shampoo for the last few days. Reaching for my shampoo, I squirt a huge dollop into my palm and bring it to the top of my head. My fingers get to work spreading and massaging it in when a stray glop slides down my forehead and into my eyeball.

Dear God, it burns! I squeal and rub at my eye, forgetting my hands are covered in the stuff.

"Shiiiittttttt!" I scream. *Too much; I used too much.* Tears are streaming down my cheeks when I try to pry my eye open under the shower spray to wash it out.

The bathroom door flies open with a bang, startling me so much I jump. The tub floor is slippery as shit from all the shampoo, so down I go in a mass of flailing arms and legs.

"Fuck! Are you okay?" Rhett is saying from above me. His hair is wet and hanging in his eyes, droplets of water streaming over his head.

I blink up at him. "What?" I'm so confused. One minute I'm washing my hair, the next I'm horizontal with a fully clothed and very wet Rhett in the shower with me. "What happened?" I ask him, dazed. *Did I hit my head?* It hurts.

Lifting my hand to rub my forehead, my fingers meet suds. I close my eyes and shake my head slowly. Why do these things keep happening to me?

Rhett

IF FULLY CLOTHED REAGAN IS HARD FOR ME TO resist, let's just say naked Reagan is almost impossible. It's the flash of pain in her eyes as she runs her fingers over her scalp that stops me from doing something stupid, like kissing her.

I swallow. Beautiful isn't a strong enough word to describe the woman splayed out before me. She is perfect. There is nothing I would change about her. Not one single thing.

Smiling down at her, I ask, "You think you can sit up now?" I'm careful not to let my eyes linger too long where they shouldn't.

She licks her wet lips. "Yeah, I think so."

Wrapping my hands around her bare shoulders, I help pull her into a sitting position. Her wet hair hangs around her, full of suds, and it dawns on me what must have happened. "You got shampoo in your eye?"

Biting down on her bottom lip, she nods then looks up at me. Her left eye is red and angry-looking. "Honey," I murmur, cupping her jaw in my palm. Her skin is slick and soapy, and I have to remind myself that she's hurt.

"Here," I say, "turn around." She brings her knees to her chest, and I take her shoulders in my hands again, then help spin her. "Close your eyes," I instruct as I gently tilt her chin back so her head is partially under the shower spray.

Moving so my legs are in the tub, I sit on the edge and run my hands through her hair, removing the shampoo. Once it's all out, I put some of her conditioner in my palm and spread it evenly through her long locks. Silky strands slide between my fingers and she sighs.

Her arms curl around her knees, and her head hangs back, resting in my hands. It feels surreal sitting here, washing her hair. I've never done anything like this before. It strikes me that this moment feels more intimate than any other I've shared with a woman before.

Sex is about mutual satisfaction. But this... this is all about her. She's so vulnerable. Yet, here she is, giving me her trust. My chest constricts with emotions I don't know how to handle.

I clear my throat. "There you go. All done," I tell her, removing my hands from her head and getting out of the way. I find a stack of towels on a shelf in the corner, grab one for her, then help her out of the tub. When I'm sure she's stable, I release her and take a step away.

Turning my back, I tug my sopping shirt over my head and drop it on the floor, then I remove my wet jeans and kick them into the corner with my shirt. I hear her sharp intake of breath behind me, and my cock stiffens. I grit my teeth and yank a towel from the rack, wrap it around my waist, then stalk out of the room because, God, do I want to turn around and devour her.

Fifteen minutes later, I'm sitting on the couch, flicking through Reagan's Netflix list, when she emerges.

"Guess we're even now," she says as she sits next to me but doesn't get too close.

My eyes slide across to her, and my cheek ticks as I smirk. "You didn't need to go to all that trouble just to make us even, you know."

Her elbow shoots out and jabs me in the ribs. "You wish."

And just like that, we're back to normal.

Thank God, because I am not ready for whatever the fuck I was feeling in that bathroom.

Our dinner arrives a few minutes later, and we settle in on her couch, watching some ridiculous British TV series about a fictional royal family while stuffing our faces with pizza.

"Cyrus is a dodgy little prick," Reagan says, bringing me up to speed on who is who and what is going on.

I don't really care, but the animated look she gets on her face as she watches makes it all worth it. I nod along as she rattles on about a second son and a secretly good bodyguard pretending to be an arsehole.

I'm ashamed to say, by the third episode, I'm getting into it. It does help that Liz Hurley plays the queen. She is smokin'. But she's got nothing on the girl curled into my side right now. *Wait, when did that happen?*

At some point, Reagan ended up snuggled against me, her head resting against my chest, while my arm has found its way around her waist. My fingers trace up and down her side and she sighs, until I feel her body completely relax. Glancing down, I realise she's fallen asleep.

Hair falls across her face, and my fingers itch to touch it. So I do. I run the glossy blonde strands through my fingertips, then tuck some of it back behind her ear. Lifting her upper body, I try to slide out from beneath her, but she groans and locks her arms tightly around my chest and snuggles in deeper.

My eyes drift over the couch; it's wide enough for the both of us. *Fuck it.* I can't believe I'm doing it, even as my legs rise up to the cushions. I shuffle my body down to lie beside her. Through it all, she remains asleep and wrapped around me.

I close my eyes and inhale her scent; it's as sweet as she is. And that's my last thought as I drift off to sleep with Reagan in my arms.

Chapter Eleven

Reagan

SOMETHING IS POKING ME IN THE BUTT. Something hard. I wriggle, trying to dislodge whatever it is, but it's no use.

My eyes pop open when I register the warm, solid chest pressed against my back. Turning my head, I come face-to-chest with Rhett. *Oh my God.* My gaze roves down our tangled bodies and widens when I see that the towel he was wearing while we were watching TV has fallen off through the night.

It's his penis poking my butt. His huge, beautiful penis. I wriggle again on instinct. I want to be closer to it. Then, his name pops into my mind—Prince Everhard of the Netherlands—and I nearly lose it. My hand flies up to cover my mouth in an attempt to stifle my laughter as my body shudders with it.

"Stop rubbing up on my cock, Reagan," Rhett grumbles in a deliciously husky tone.

It sends a shiver down my spine, and I squirm. "Sorry," I whisper.

"You will be if you don't stay fucking still," he says, all traces of sleep gone from his voice as his hands grip my hips. His fingertips dig into my flesh, and I love it.

I know he's telling me to stop, but I can't help it. The combination of his stern words, his hard grip on me, and his throbbing cock pressed so close to where I want it is too much. My hips wriggle against his hold all on their own.

"Reagan," he growls.

I'm so turned on right now it's unbearable. "I'm sorry," I say again, "I can't help it. You feel so good."

His breath comes out hot, hard, and fast against the back of my neck, and I swallow as his hands squeeze my hips harder.

"Fuck it," he says, then his lips press to my neck, sucking as he pulls my hips back into his hard-on with so much force I moan.

One of his hands snakes around to my centre, and he roughly shoves my underwear aside then slides his finger through my folds. My whole body shudders. "Oh God, yes."

"I tried, Reagan. I tried really fucking hard to keep my hands off you."

"I know," I pant as his finger presses inside me. "I'm sorry," I cry as my back arches into his touch.

"Stop me, Reagan. Stop me right now, and I'll go home and fuck my own fist until I come to thoughts of your sweet little pussy wrapped around my aching cock. Tell me to stop," he pleads against my throat.

But I can't. I want it too much. I want *him* too much.

His lips never leave my flesh for longer than a second. His finger pumps inside me in time with his hips pushing into me from behind, and my inner muscles tighten. One of my hands wraps around his wrist, keeping him in place, as my other glides up around his neck and locks in the hair at his nape.

He moans, "Fuck, honey, so tight and wet for me."

All I can do is nod as I'm overtaken by sensation. It starts deep inside—a sweet tingle that emanates outward until I'm shuddering and convulsing in his arms. "Rhett," I cry as my orgasm takes me away.

I'm floating down from the best climax I've ever had when his hand slides out of my pants and tugs them down my legs. He lifts my thigh, spreading me, then thrusts forward.

His knob touches my opening, and I shudder

again. "Yes," I breathe, suddenly desperate to have all of him inside me. I push my hips back.

"Condom?" he asks.

"My room," I tell him.

Then, he's swooping me up in his strong arms and throwing me over his shoulder as he stalks towards my bedroom. I watch his gorgeous arse as he walks and grin like a fool with my knickers hanging around my ankles.

Rhett

I'm not thinking straight. I know I'm not, but how can I with her in my arms?

The second I'm close enough, I drop her to her bed. She bounces once, then shimmies her way up the mattress, losing her panties as she goes, her eyes never leaving mine.

"Top drawer," she says, using her chin to gesture to her bedside.

Yanking it open, I find a brand-new box and rip it apart. Her eyes sparkle as she watches me slide the condom down my shaft. She's practically glowing under my gaze. Climbing over her, I slide my hands under the hem of her top, pushing it up her perfect breasts then over her head.

My breath catches in my throat at the sight of the intricate vine tattooed around her torso. I hadn't seen it when she changed her top in front of me that first day, and I didn't take the time to examine it in the tub last night. But now, I'm mesmerised by it. Reaching out, I trace its path from her hip bone, up her ribs, around the underside of her breast, then to the point where it twists back and disappears at her side. Blue, purple, and yellow flowers sprout from the vine, some in bloom, some still just buds. It's delicate and beautiful.

"You like it?" she asks, drawing my attention back to her face.

"I fucking love it."

Her smile is blinding, and I have to kiss her. Not like the other day. No. I need to kiss her properly. Dropping down to my elbows, I hover a mere inch from her mouth. "I've wanted to do this since I first saw you standing in your doorway, clutching that hammer and wearing those frilly pink shorts."

"Really?" Her eyes shimmer with uncertainty.

I nod. "And the more time I spend with you, the harder it is to stop myself. But I can't stop this time, Reagan. I need to taste you like I need my next breath."

She swallows, then tips her chin up, offering me her mouth. I close the space, softly grazing my lips over hers once, twice, three times, then slide my tongue over her plump bottom lip. Her mouth parts on a breath, and I deepen the kiss.

Her fingers glide up my biceps, over my shoulders, up my neck, and over my scalp. I groan when her hands tighten into fists in my hair. She squirms beneath me, and our bodies align perfectly. Parting her legs further, she invites me in. And I don't hesitate, thrusting my hips forward until I'm buried balls deep in her warmth.

She whimpers, and I still.

"I'm sorry, honey. I should have gone slow," I murmur against her cheek, feeling like an arsehole for taking her so fast. I'm big and I know better than to ram in like that.

Surprising me, she shakes her head. "No, no, it's good. So good. Don't stop now."

I smile down at her. "You are somethin' else, Reagan."

She grins back. "A good something or a bad something?" she asks, mimicking our conversation from earlier in the week.

"Definitely a good something," I assure her, then kiss the shit out of her.

She comes twice more before I can no longer

hold my own orgasm in check. I throw my head back as I come harder than I have in all my life. Dropping to her side, I tug her over to me, wrapping my arm around her as we catch our breath.

"Did you know that coffee drinkers have sex more frequently than non-coffee drinkers?" she asks, her palm resting over my heart.

I kiss the top of her head, smiling. "And there she is—the chick who can find a random fact to complement any situation."

She laughs and snuggles in more closely. "It's a gift. Or a disability. I'm not sure which."

"A gift for sure, honey," I tell her, then slap her bare arse. "Come on. I'll help you shower, then we need to restock your fridge. There's nothing in there for breakfast."

An hour later, we've showered and had sex in the shower, then I ducked home to get fresh clothes, and Reagan is waiting for me in front of the elevator. I wrap my arm around her neck and kiss the top of her head. She smells so damn good. *Will I ever get sick of the way she smells?*

The elevator doors slide open, and I release her so she can hobble in on her crutches. "Where do you normally get your groceries?" she asks as we descend to the basement parking lot.

I shrug. "Wherever's closest when I realise I

need them. Is there a particular store you want to go to?"

"No, I don't mind where we go. Seen one supermarket, seen them all." She smiles at me.

Nodding, I tell her, "I know of one a few blocks away; it'll do."

Pulling into a parking spot, I jump out of my ute and grin when my eyes land on a disability shopping cart. I go get it and bring it around to her side of the truck, looking at her expectantly.

She looks down at it and shakes her head. "Uh, no."

Frowning, I gesture to the padded seat in front of me. "Come on now, you don't really want to try getting through the whole shop on those crutches. You need a lot of stuff. We're going to be a while."

Her shoulders slump. "Fine," she grumbles, then holds her arms out for me to help her.

We're in the fresh produce section when she pipes up. "I can see the advantage of this contraption now."

Glancing down at her, I raise a brow at the cheeky glint in her eyes. "Oh yeah? What's that?"

"I'm at eye level with Prince Everhard. He and I can have a conversation while you do the groceries."

I choke on air. "Ah, what? You're insane, you know that?"

Now she raises a brow at me. "You're just figuring that out now? A little slow, aren't you?"

Rolling my eyes, I turn my attention back to the vegetables, then grab some baby broccoli and asparagus to go with our breakfast when we get home. *Wait, home? Am I planning on going back to her place when we're done?*

Umm, fuck yes, I am. And that thought should produce fear in me. But for some bizarre reason, it doesn't. Having sex hasn't changed anything between us. Reagan's still her random self, and I don't have the urge to run as far away as possible.

Maybe we could work after all?

Reagan

"HELLO, EARTH TO REAGAN?" RHETT SNAPS HIS fingers in front of my face, making me startle.

I glare at him. "What?"

He shakes his head, smirking at me. "I was asking what kind of ice cream you like? You were spaced out, staring at my dick."

Heat blooms in my cheeks. "Oh, umm, cookies and cream."

I was totally staring at his penis. Well, not like, directly at it. I'd have to open his pants to do that, and I'm pretty sure the other shoppers would not appreciate that. Not the male ones anyway; I've seen more than a few of my fellow female shoppers running their greedy little eyes over Rhett's magnificent assets.

I don't blame them. I used to look at him all the time when I'd pass him in the foyer of our building. Or when we'd share the elevator. I'm sure I looked like a total creeper, though, since discretion has never been my strong suit.

"You're doing it again," he says.

I roll my eyes. "So? What's your point?"

He snorts. "People are going to think you're a bit special—your eyes all glazed over, staring at my crotch. And I think there's a bit of drool just here," he says, running his thumb over my bottom lip. Using his pointer fingers, he tilts my head back then bends down and presses a kiss to my lips. "Lucky for you, I kinda like your brand of special," he whispers against my ear, then winks when he straightens and goes back to pushing the cart down the aisle.

My cheeks hurt from smiling so much. I'm a happy-go-lucky kind of person—I normally smile a lot—but this week I've broken a record. *Why didn't I just introduce myself to him when I moved into the building? Why?!*

After just one week, I'm already fully in like with him.

I bite my lip. *Slow down, Reagan. He made it clear where he stands on dating. You're setting yourself up for heartbreak.*

Rhett

REAGAN HAS BEEN UNUSUALLY QUIET SINCE WE got back in the truck. It's worrying me. "You okay? Your foot hurting?"

She shakes her head. "No, I'm okay. Tired, maybe. We stayed up pretty late, then we rose crazy early this morning. Plus, the exercise. I'm not used to that much physical activity," she says, smiling.

This smile lacks the punch that usually accompanies her true smiles. Something is bothering her. Should I push her to tell me or let it go?

Before I can decide, she says, "Did you know thirty thousand people are seriously injured from exercise equipment each year? True fact. Scary fact, if you ask me. That's the reason I have never set foot in a gym. No, sir. Not this little blonde duck."

I frown. "Blonde duck?"

She nods and shuffles around on the seat until her back's pressed to the door and she's facing me. "Yeah, you know the saying, *'not this little black duck'*? Well, I'm blonde, so duh."

"You're a crack-up. Have you ever considered a career in stand-up comedy?" I think she'd rock it. All she'd have to do is get up there and be herself. She'd be a hit.

Her nose scrunches adorably. "Umm, no. Have you seen the clothes those women wear? Not once have I seen a decently dressed stand-up act. Not once. If I even thought about wearing those kinds of clothes"—she pauses as a shudder runs over her—"Char would shoot me."

"That's a bit rough."

Reagan widens her eyes at me. "It's true. Think about it. Have you ever seen an attractive stand-up? It's like a job requirement to be dowdy. Or maybe it's what the job does to you? Like, they could have been perfectly good-looking, then they became comedians and boom."

I laugh at her antics. She's being completely serious right now, and that makes it even funnier.

"And why would your friend want to shoot you for becoming average-looking?"

Her cheek lifts in a sneer. "That's if I didn't shoot myself first. I have standards, you know. And have you ever heard of Charlotte's Closet? It's the most popular fashion blog in the country. That's my Charlotte."

Now that I think about it, I do remember my sister going on about something like that. "Yeah, I think Piper follows it. But I'm not exactly a fashionista, in case you hadn't noticed."

Reagan's eyes roam over me. And just like that, the punch that was missing from her smile before is right back again. "You do just fine. You could wear a paper bag and you'd still be sex on a stick."

I burst out laughing. "What does that even mean?"

She grins. "I'll show you when we get back to the apartment."

My foot presses down a little harder on the accelerator.

Chapter Twelve

Reagan

The rest of Saturday was a blur of amazing sex, incredible orgasms, delicious food, and binge-watching Netflix. In other words, absolute perfection.

I squint as the sunlight peeks through my curtains. *It's morning already?* Lifting my hand, I rub the sleep from my eyes. It feels like we only just fell into bed. But as I focus on my alarm clock, I'm shocked that it's eleven a.m.

Reaching out, my hand slaps about on my bedside table until it comes into contact with my phone. Scooping it up, I swipe my finger across the screen when I see two missed calls from Char and a few texts from her and my dad, too.

I shoot Dad a quick reply, then open the first message from Char that reads:

CHARLOTTE: Bitch where are you? I called! I never call!

It's true; we aren't the phone call types unless it's an emergency—like my mini-meltdown earlier in the week. Her next message is a little more aggressive:

CHARLOTTE: Woman, you better be dead because I called TWICE!

And her third and most recent:

CHARLOTTE: Okay, I've had time to think it over, and I've decided you're dead to me. That's right. You just lost the best thing that ever happened to you. I hope you're happy.

Pfft, and she thinks I'm the dramatic one of the two of us. *Please.*

Rhett's arms squeeze my middle. "Why are you awake?"

My fingers are flying across the screen when I answer him. "Sun woke me up; it's after eleven. And Char is having a nervous breakdown because I haven't answered her calls."

He nuzzles his face in my neck and breathes deeply. "Okay, you deal with that. I'm going to sleep. You wore me out, you little sex fiend." Then he presses his lips to my throat, and all of a sudden, I'm thinking about sex again.

I wriggle my arse against his morning wood. "Don't act like you don't like it."

"Never said I didn't." He chuckles, then moves his head back up to rest on the pillow beside mine, keeping his arms wrapped securely around me.

Shaking my head, I drag my attention back to my phone.

ME: Settle down, psycho. I've been wrapped up in an orgasm-fest. I'll call you later.

Little dots appear immediately on my screen, signalling Char's imminent reply.

CHARLOTTE: You dirty little whore! I want details right damn now. You can't say orgasm-fest, then not share the deets.

ME: So your sexy-time sensors weren't as far off as I thought they were …

CHARLOTTE: I KNEW IT! Tell me everything. Every filthy little detail. I need it all. You know how long it's been for me.

ME: Can't I just call you later? I'm in bed with him right now. He's sleeping next to me.

CHARLOTTE: I need photographic evidence.

Licking my lips, I lift my head to check if Rhett has fallen back to sleep or not yet. And yep, he's out. With sloth-like slowness, I lift my phone above us and snap a selfie, belatedly realising my phone isn't on silent. *Shit.*

"Did you just take a picture of me?" Rhett asks, his eyes still closed.

"Huh? Uh, no. What a weird thing to ask," I deflect.

"Then why did your phone just make the camera shutter sound?"

Shit! When in doubt, use half-truths to sound convincing. "I was taking a selfie... for Char."

"You just took a naked picture of yourself for your friend?" His eyes remain closed, and he doesn't sound phased by any of this.

"No. The sheet is covering all the important bits," I tell him.

"Can I see it?" he asks, then he's on top of me, pinning me beneath his big body, a wolfish grin covering his mouth, showing me his white teeth.

I squeal, "No! It's private!"

With everything I have, I fight him, trying to keep my phone out of his grasp. And with a pathetic amount of effort, he snatches it from me. Looking at the screen, he grins, taps it a few times, then hands it back to me. He rolls to the side, wraps his arm back around my waist, and makes himself comfortable again.

"What did you do?" I ask when I see there are no signs of vandalism on the picture staring back at me.

"I sent it to myself, then your friend, with the caption *'he has a huge cock'*."

I snort with laughter and check my sent messages. Sure enough, the little dots in Char's message window are flashing away.

CHARLOTTE: You tease. You didn't need to be in it. And you could have moved the sheet down a few inches. I can tell he's hard under there, but an unobstructed view would be preferable.

Closing my eyes, I shake my head at my best friend. "She's as big a perv as you are. She's requesting a photo, sans sheet and me."

Rhett chuckles beside me. "Not happening; I don't do dick pics. And if I did, I wouldn't be sending them to your friend."

Rolling into his side, I kiss his cheek. "I'm glad to

hear it. And just so you know, I wouldn't be opposed to receiving them," I whisper against his ear, then suck the lobe into my mouth.

His hands move down to my arse and drag me on top of him until I can feel him between my legs. I throw my phone over my shoulder and move my mouth back to his.

Rhett

She is insatiable; it's fucking awesome.

We spent the whole weekend between her bed and the couch. Now, it's Monday morning, and the last thing I want to do is leave the warmth of her small body tucked into mine. But it's time to return to real life.

She's sleeping soundly, and I do my best not to disturb her as I slide out from behind her and collect my clothes off the floor. Tugging my jeans up, I head for the door.

"You going already?" Her husky sleep-filled voice hits my back.

Glancing at her over my shoulder, I'm struck by just how perfect she is. I can't go without kissing her one last time. Striding to her, I kneel on the side of the bed, brush her hair out of her face, and press my lips to hers. She's so sweet, so pliant under my touch, so perfect.

Her hands snake up into my hair, holding me to her. "Stay a little longer," she whispers.

God, do I want to.

Using her grip on my head, she lifts her upper body to mine, pressing her bare tits into my chest. Her nipples pebble, and my hand slides between us, plucking one between my fingertips. My decision is made; I can't leave without one more taste. I'm the fucking boss—if I want to come in late, I will.

Reagan's hands leave my hair. Digging her nails in, she scrapes them down my back, then slides them into my pants, squeezing my arse. She really does love my arse. I grin into her mouth. Then, she's tugging on my zipper and shoving my jeans down my thighs.

"You've turned me into a sex-crazed maniac." She chuckles when she can't get my pants off quick enough. She hooks her good foot into the fabric gathered at my knees and pushes, trying to force it down.

I lose my balance over her and topple off the side of the bed. She's on top of me in seconds, eyes alight with need. Her hand slaps around blindly on the bedside table, her gaze never leaving mine. She grins wickedly and produces a condom, holding it in two fingers between us.

Snatching it from her, I rip it open with my teeth, then slide it down my shaft. I'm so fucking hard; I'm aching to be inside her.

As soon as the condom is in place, she positions herself above me and lowers her sweet pussy onto my cock. My muscles clench as she takes her time sliding down until she's fully seated, then she rocks her hips back and forth.

My fingers sink into her flesh, and I jack knife up, sucking one of her nipples into my mouth. Her hands are back in my hair, gripping it in her tiny fists as she rides me. Nothing has ever felt better.

I move my mouth to her other nipple, and she moans. I suck harder, then let it pop from my mouth and bite down on her lush tit. It's going to mark her, and I love knowing she will be carrying the imprint of my teeth with her when we're apart.

Her movements lose their rhythm, she clenches around me, and I have to grit my teeth, holding back. I help her get there, moving her hips for her as I suck on her throat. Seconds later, she's shuddering, whimpering, and coming all over my cock, and I come with her.

We stay like that on her bedroom floor for I don't

know how long, until Reagan tugs my head back by my hair. Her eyes sparkle like sapphires. She lightly runs her nose over mine, then her lips whisper over my cheeks.

"Are we okay?" she breathes across my parted lips.

I swallow. I knew this was coming. The talk. I have no fucking clue what to say. I can't remember ever being this happy, this comfortable with a chick, this content. "I think so," I tell her honestly. That's the best I can give her right now.

Resting her forehead against mine, she breathes, "Okay."

She doesn't seem angry or annoyed with my less-than-confident reply. I'm not sure if that's a good thing or a bad thing.

STRIDING INTO THE SHOP AN HOUR AFTER opening, I ignore Jake and Taj's stares and go straight into the break room. I need more caffeine.

Jake follows me—the prick. "Where were you this morning, big man?"

I flip him off. "None of your fucking business."

The arrogant bastard grabs a chair, swings it around, and sits on it backwards, arms crossed over the top as he stares at me. "You've been in a good mood recently," he says, then raises a brow. "Who is she?"

I turn my back to him and go about making my coffee. "Don't know what you're talking about."

To make matters worse, the door swings open with a bang against the wall. "Where the fuck have you been? Jessie had a meltdown yesterday because you weren't at the fucking rehearsal dinner." Simon is in my face, shoving at my chest.

I frown. *Rehearsal dinner?* "What are you talking about? The wedding isn't for two weeks."

His eyes are feral. "I told you we had to do the rehearsal dinner early because Jess was freaking out about the catering. Don't you listen to anything I say? You're supposed to be my best man, and where were you? Off fucking some bimbo?"

My fist launches into his jaw before I even know what I'm doing. *Shit!* "Simon! Fuck. I'm sorry, man. I didn't mean—"

"You son of a bitch," he yells, wrapping his hands around my throat.

I swing my arms up from below and break his apart, loosening his grip, then shove him away. "I said I was sorry."

He paces back and forth but says nothing, his fists clenching and unclenching at his sides.

Jake just sits there watching, not bothering to get in between us. Smart man. This isn't the first scuffle Simon and I have had in here, and no doubt, it won't be the last. He's my best friend. Who's going to pull us into line, if not each other?

Once Simon's calmed down, he straightens his shirt and runs his hands through his hair. "So, where were you? What was more important than being there for me?"

Rubbing the back of my neck, I look at my boots. "I forgot. I'm sorry, man. I ah ..." I swallow. "I was with someone."

Simon balks. "Someone? That's it? That's all I get? You missed my rehearsal dinner, Rhett. I'm going to need more than that."

I don't know what this thing with Reagan is yet. I don't want to tell Simon about her. Hell, I have no idea what I would even say. *Oh, hey man, I completely forgot about your rehearsal dinner because I was screwing my trippy little neighbour girl all weekend. She's awesome, and funny, and fucking perfect.*

I'm not prepared to answer the inevitable questions that would come after that little confession. So, I lie to my best friend. "I fucked up. I'm sorry. It won't happen again. Whatever you need, man, I'll be there."

He narrows his eyes. "I don't believe you."

I shrug. "What do you want me to say?"

"I want you to tell me the truth. This isn't like you missing my mum's birthday party. This shit's important."

Cracking my neck, I fix my gaze on him. "Fine. Fuck. Okay, I was with my neighbour, Reagan. She hurt herself last weekend, and I've been helping her out."

Simon's brows raise. "You were ... helping her out?"

I nod. "Yeah." Dropping my eyes, I rub the back of my neck again. "It was kinda my fault she got hurt. So, I've been checking in on her, making sure she's getting on alright. And we ended up spending the weekend together."

Tilting his head, he sizes me up. "You've been checking in on her and spent the weekend with her?" Then his face splits with a grin. "You like her. After all these years, you've finally found a woman."

My head is shaking, and I can't stop it. "She's just a cool chick, is all. It's not a big deal."

He smirks. "It's a huge fucking deal. So, are you bringing her to the wedding?"

What the fuck? Where did that even come from? I stare at him like he's lost his damn mind.

"What? You think I'm going to let you screw this

up? Oh no, my friend. I'm going to make sure this chick hangs around. You've already put in more time with her than any other woman you've ever met. You checked in on her all week and spent the weekend with her; you've got it bad." He claps me on the shoulder and heads for the door.

He's gone before I can get my thoughts in order, and Jake is grinning like a fool. "Don't you have a job to do?" I snap at him, then snatch my coffee off the sink, spilling it over my hand as I storm out to the work bays.

Chapter Thirteen

Reagan

I got a few curious stares as I hobbled around the Pink Bits offices on my bedazzled crutches. But I had way too much on my plate to worry about funny looks. An issue had come up over the weekend with the submission tool on the website, so I was busy dealing with that all day.

By the time I get home, I just want to curl up and sleep for a week. Rhett and I didn't sleep nearly enough over the weekend, and now I'm really feeling it.

Sinking onto the couch, I drop my crutches and bag on the floor then snuggle into one of my many throw pillows. It doesn't take long for sleep to take me.

I wake with a start. My phone is ringing loudly in my bag, and I reach for it, rolling off the couch in the process. My face breaks my fall with a thud. *Ow.* I rub my sore cheek and pull my phone out. "Hello."

"Hi. Listen, you don't know me. My name is Simon. I'm Rhett's best friend."

The mention of Rhett has me jerking upright, and my head spins from the rapid movement. "Is he okay?"

"Oh, yeah, no, he's fine, he's fine. Look, I'm just calling to invite you to my wedding. It's next Saturday. I know what Rhett's like at remembering shit and figured I'd just call and ask you myself."

Holding my smarting cheek, I pull my phone away from my ear to stare at the screen. Am I awake right now, or is this a weird dream? Placing it back against my face, I ask, "How did you get my number?"

The man on the other end chuckles. "I had to be resourceful. When Rhett mentioned you this morning, I went back to his apartment building and checked the name registry. I knew you were his neighbour, and that your name is Reagan, so I just needed your last name, Miss Moore, then I was able to Google your number."

I scrunch my face up. *That's a lot of effort to get my number.* "Okay, that's kinda creepy, but I guess it sort of makes sense. I still don't understand why you're inviting me to your wedding, though."

He sighs. "Rhett is going to do something to screw things up with you. I've known him my whole life. And not since we were seniors in high school has he spent more than a single night with a woman. But he said he was with you all weekend. You have to realise what a big deal that is."

Rhett's words from Thursday morning run through my head: *I don't do girlfriends. I don't date. I don't hang out. That's just not me, Reagan.* My eyes sting because I can't help but hope our time together means as much to him as it does to me. But I have to be realistic. "I'm not trying to make him something he's not," I tell his friend. "If he wants me to come to your wedding, he can ask me himself."

"I guess I can respect that," Simon mutters. "Just … can you do something for me, please?"

I lick my dry lips. "Maybe. Depends what it is."

"Whatever he does next, don't take it to heart. He has hang-ups that he needs to work through. Can you just—I don't know—keep that in mind for me?"

I'm nodding, then I realise he can't see me. "Yeah, I can do that."

"Thanks. I'm really looking forward to meeting you, Reagan," Simon says, and he sounds genuine.

"Umm, thanks?"

He chuckles. "Okay, well, I'll be seeing you. Hopefully." Then he hangs up.

Well, that was strange and unexpected. Getting off the floor, I make my way to my bedroom, too tired and confused by that phone call to even bother having a shower. I strip off and crawl into bed.

The next time I wake, it's to sunlight streaming through my curtains. I roll out of bed and shuffle to the shower.

I half expect Rhett to show up for breakfast, but he doesn't. I wait an extra half hour before finally making my morning coffee. He isn't coming.

We didn't make any plans yesterday morning after we parted ways. Maybe that was his way of ending things. But why get my number if he was just going to drop out of my life two days later?

My traitorous emotions get the better of me, and my eyes prickle right before a few tears escape. I sniffle and scrub them away—I refuse to cry about this. We had a really good time together. I won't regret it. I won't. Even if I wish it wasn't over.

Rhett

I WANTED TO GO TO HER LAST NIGHT. BUT I didn't.

Instead, I went to the pub and ended up nursing the same beer for two hours before I slid it back across the bar and left. I didn't go home, though. I couldn't.

My sister's couch is nowhere near as comfortable as Reagan's. And her coffee mugs are boring as shit. I scowl down at the plain purple mug in my hands, wishing it had some smart-arse quote on it.

"Okay, I let you sleep on my couch, and I didn't ask any questions. But now I want answers. You're even more grumpy than you usually are in the mornings. What's going on?" Piper asks, standing on the other side of her kitchen table, hands on her hips, presumably waiting for me to spill my guts.

Averting my gaze from her expectant glare, I look out the kitchen window. "Nothing. My air conditioner is broken. I just needed somewhere to crash that wasn't a sauna. I'll get it fixed this week."

She says nothing, but I hear the distinct sound of her tapping her foot against the floorboards. Glancing back at her, I know she's not buying my story, even though it's partially true.

I sigh. "Okay, I'm avoiding my neighbour. Don't worry, it'll blow over in a day or two, and I'll be out of your hair."

She cocks a brow. Her electric-blue-streaked hair falls around her shoulders as she leans over the table, bracing her hands on it. "You're a shit liar. That's why you always got busted when you pulled stupid pranks as a kid, and I got away with murder."

Jesus Christ. Why can't I just figure this shit out on my own without everyone trying to make me talk it out?

I scrub the back of my neck and stare into my coffee. "We might have hooked up over the weekend, and now I just need a bit of space. It's not a big deal, Piper. Let it go."

Piper's jaw drops. "Since when do you actively avoid hook-ups? You've never had a problem telling women it was a one-time deal. What's different about this one?" she asks, dragging the chair opposite me out from under the table and taking a seat.

"She's different. It didn't start as a hook-up. We hung out a few times, and it progressed." I shrug. "Now I don't know what to fucking do."

My little sister blinks at me dumbly. "You go with it, you moron. I haven't seen you interested in anyone since Meghan cheated on you in high school. That was ten years ago, Rhett. That's a long time to let one person dictate your life."

I know she's right. What happened with Meghan really screwed me up. I thought I loved her. I saw it all in my head: we'd get married, I'd finish my apprenticeship and open my own garage, then we'd have a couple of kids.

Yeah, I was that guy. I was Simon. All full of hope and big dreams for the future. Then, I walked in on Meghan blowing my fellow teammate, and it all went up in flames. I haven't pictured a future involving another woman since.

After that, I ploughed through women like I was born to do it, making up for the two years I had been faithful to Meghan. Well, I went through as many as would take me, that is. The amount who saw the size of my junk and offered me a handy or blowjob instead is ridiculous.

"Rhett." Piper's quiet voice pulls my attention back to her.

"What?"

"Meghan was a mole. End of story. But you've been letting her determine the outcome of your life for far too long. She's in your past, but you've been carrying her around all this time. What's this new girl like? Tell me about her."

The shadow that creeps in when I think of what Meghan put me through is superseded by the light I feel whenever I'm around Reagan.

"She's funny, even though she doesn't always mean to be. She's really accident-prone. In just a few days, she stepped on two shards of glass, tripped on her own feet, and fell off a bar stool." I shake my head thinking of her. "She's easy-going and super chill, has a vendetta against bras, and lacks a filter."

Piper smiles. "She sounds pretty awesome to me. What's her name?"

"Reagan." Just saying her name out loud makes me miss her even more. It's a foreign feeling for me. Actually, everything I feel about her is foreign to me. I really don't like it.

After Meghan, I promised myself I would never allow my happiness to be reliant on another person. And look at me now; I'm miserable, and it's only been twenty-four hours since I was with Reagan.

My head throbs. I don't want to think about this anymore. I simply want to go back to the way things have always been. It's safe, satisfying, and headache free.

Piper's warm hand curls around my wrist. "Why are you fighting it? You obviously like her, and the look in your eyes when you talk about her tells me everything I need to know. I think you should see where this goes, Rhett. Give her a chance."

I swallow past the lump in the base of my throat. "I'll think about it." Catching sight of the time on the wall clock, I push my chair back. "I gotta go, big day at the shop today."

"Okay, I'll call you later," Piper says, going up on her tippy-toes to kiss my cheek before I leave.

When I walk into my garage, Jake and Taj stay out of my way. Jesus, I must look as bad as I feel if those two aren't giving me shit for being late two days in a row. I make myself another coffee, then get to work. I've got a vintage Cadi waiting for me today, and I plan on losing myself in her all day long.

Reagan

ANOTHER DAY OF RADIO SILENCE FROM RHETT, and I'm driving myself mad with worry. Is he okay? Did something happen to him? Is that why he hasn't checked in the last two days?

Chewing on my bottom lip, I decide it's time to call in Char. She will know what to do. Hitting her name on my phone screen, I wait for her to answer.

"S'up, sugar tits?" she greets in a super chipper tone.

My shoulders slump before I even start talking. "Char, he's dropped off the face of the Earth. I haven't seen or heard from him since Monday morning. Everything was fine—no, it was great. We went our separate ways when we left for work, and that was the last time I saw him. Is this him ghosting me, or was he murdered by psychotic dwarfs?"

"Whoa, slow down, babe," she says, and I take a breath, trying to calm myself.

"Okay, so it's Wednesday night, and you're panicking because it's been crickets since Monday. Correct?"

"Yeah," I breathe. "I mean, he told me he didn't do girlfriends or anything. Then the weekend happened, and I don't know, I thought ..." I can't finish my sentence because I'm not sure what I thought.

"Oh, babe," Char coos. "I'll be over in half an hour with wine and chocolate."

"Thank you," I whisper and end the call.

My work clothes feel too tight, so I start tugging them off on my way to my room. I'm able to get around without my crutches now if I'm careful. I'm naked when I reach my closet, and I grab the first pair of jammies I see, yanking them on. Then, I flop back on my bed and wait for Char to arrive.

Almost exactly thirty minutes later, my apartment door bangs open, and Char's voice sings out, "Honey, I'm home!"

I don't bother getting up. "I'm in here," I call out.

A couple of seconds later, she leans against the doorframe. She's got two bottles of wine tucked under her arm and a bag that I'm sure is full of chocolate swinging from her wrist.

I smile at her. "Lifesaver."

She throws the bag of chocolate to me, then drops her purse on the floor and kicks off her shoes. "I'll get us some glasses. Be right back," she says with a wink, then she disappears.

We're sitting side by side in my bed, leaning against the headboard with a bottle of wine each. *This is what best friends are for.*

CHAR ENDED UP GOING HOME AND PACKING A bag so she could stay with my sorry arse for the rest of the week. It's not like me to mope, but Rhett is worth moping over.

We're in my bed, where we've spent every night after finishing work with wine, chocolate and pretzels. I'm staring at the ceiling, wishing my phone would ring. Hell, at this point I'd even be happy with a text. But nada. I haven't so much as seen a glimpse of him since Monday morning.

Char smacks her forehead with her palm, and I give her the side eye. "I can't believe I haven't already asked this, but when did you first text him?"

I look at her, confused. "I haven't."

Her red lips pop open in a perfect O. "Not even just a 'Hey, thanks for the great sex' or a 'You're an arsehole with a tiny penis' text?"

Shaking my head, I tell her, "Firstly, nothing on that man is tiny, especially his epic penis. And secondly, I didn't know I was supposed to."

She scoffs. "Give me your phone. We're fixing this right now."

Before I can stop her, she snatches my phone off the quilt, and she's tapping away on my screen.

"Hey! What are you going to say?" I screech, my arms helicoptering, trying to reclaim my phone.

Char rolls her eyes and stands up on the bed, then holds it above her head. She's almost a foot taller than me, the cow.

"I can't find his name in your contacts," she complains.

I grin, victorious. "And you won't. It's not in there under his real name."

A minute later, she busts out laughing. She buckles in half, then drops to her knees as tears stream down her cheeks. Yep, she found his contact info. My lips quirk. It really is a good name—and very accurate.

PINK BITS

"Prince Everhard of the Netherlands ... Oh God, Reagan, why didn't you warn me?" Char pants.

I shrug. "It would've ruined the effect."

"It's fitting that a queen would end up with a prince." She giggles.

Taking several deep breaths, she shuffles back to sitting against the headboard. "Babe, you need to text him. Doesn't matter what you say; just keep it light and easy. You can do that. Give him a chance to explain himself before you start having nightmares about midgets again."

"Okay, I can do that."

Char hands my phone back, and I stare at it, praying for inspiration. Then it hits me like a freight train, and my fingers fly over the screen.

ME: More than ten people a year are killed by vending machines.

I sit back, satisfied I've done a good thing. Until Char grabs my phone to read it and starts staring at me funnily. "What?"

Her brows pinch together. "This is what you sent to the man you want to be having sex with? Babe, I'm going to be honest. I'm not sure how he's going to respond to this, if at all."

Oh. My chest deflates. "He likes it when I tell him random facts."

Char chews her lip for a moment, then her eyes widen. "Look, he's typing!" she squeals and hands me back the phone.

His response takes forever, but my eyes never leave the screen.

RHETT: Are you planning on dropping a vending machine on me in the near future?

ME: I wasn't. Should I be?

RHETT: Maybe.

I frown. I don't like that response. My chest squeezes, then my heart takes off at a gallop.

ME: Why?

RHETT: Because I've been avoiding you.

ME: Oh. You don't have to. I understand. You don't do girlfriends.

RHETT: No, you don't understand.

Chapter Fourteen

Reagan

My head whips up at the banging coming from the front of my apartment. I look at Char, who seems to be just as startled by it as me. Crawling off my bed, I go to the front door and open it cautiously.

I jump back when Rhett pushes the door open. Stalking towards me, he forces me backwards until I'm pressed against the wall. His fingers glide over my cheeks, then up into my messy hair. He tips my head back, and then he's kissing me like a man starved.

Sighing, I relax into his hold, returning his kiss with as much passion as he gives me. My arms curl around his shoulders, and he moves his hands to my butt, hoisting me up to his hips. I lock my ankles behind his back.

"I'm sorry, honey. I got buried in my past, but I'm here now," he breathes against my kiss-swollen lips.

If I wasn't tethered to him, I swear I would soar into the sky with happiness.

He's actually here. I blink back tears as my emotions rage for control. Problem is, I'm not sure which I'm feeling more: relieved that he's here, or pissed that he could have been a body in the morgue and I wouldn't even have known.

I push my hands against his solid chest. He takes the hint and lowers me to the floor, keeping his hands on my hips.

"Where have you been?" I ask, then change my mind. "No. Scratch that. What the hell took you so long?"

His answering grin is everything.

Lightly gliding his rough fingertips over my cheek, he looks deep into my eyes and says, "I had to get my head straight. I'm sorry, honey. It won't happen again; I swear. This has been the worst week of my life. I'm miserable without you."

Swallowing becomes really freaking hard, and my unshed tears spill over. It takes me a minute to gain control of my vocal cords. "Well good, because I reverted to an overly angsty teenager who eats her feelings this week, so at least we were both suffering."

"It's true. She's been moody as hell. She bit me

last night when I tried to take her fifth chocolate bar off her."

Rhett's head swivels to Char, who's leaning against my bedroom doorframe, her arms crossed under her boobs and a smug expression on her face.

"Uh, hi there. Sorry, I didn't realise there was anyone else here."

Char snorts. "That's because you were too busy sucking face with my girl. But I'll forgive you this time. That's the first smile I've seen out of her all week."

Rhett grins back at me, then kisses my nose and presses his forehead to mine. "You bit her?"

I shrug. "She knows better than to touch my chocolate. Especially when I'm in the throes of an emotional breakdown."

His expression sobers with my last statement. "Baby, I'm so sorry. I didn't mean to hurt you. My head was so far up my own arse I didn't stop to think how my silence would affect you."

"I should have called or messaged you sooner. At first, I thought you might just need some space, but then after a few days, I knew it was more than that. I thought my crazy was too much for you to handle for more than a weekend," I admit.

Running the pads of his thumbs under my eyes, he wipes away my tears. "Reagan," he says, then stops until I meet his intense gaze. "I fucking love your brand of crazy. I had more fun with you in one weekend than I've had in years. You are so much more than you give yourself credit for.

"You're crazy smart." He presses a kiss to my forehead. "Crazy beautiful." A kiss to my left cheek. "Crazy clumsy." A kiss to my right. "Crazy fun." A kiss to my nose. "And I'm fucking crazy about you." His soft lips meet mine, and I wrap my arms around his neck, never wanting this to end.

"Ahem." Char interrupts us before we can get carried away.

"Shit, sorry," I mumble. It takes me a moment to catch my breath.

Char rolls her eyes. "Well, it looks like my work here is done. I'll get my stuff and leave you two horndogs to it." She turns back to my room and gathers her things quickly.

She strides down the hall and pauses when she reaches us. Holding her hand out to Rhett, she says, "By the way, I'm Charlotte. Otherwise known as the best bitch or friend, depending what day it is. I'd say it was nice to meet you, but we haven't really had a chance to do that yet, so we'll put a pin in it and take care of the formalities some other time."

Rhett takes Char's outstretched hand. "I'm good with that."

Char's eyes roam over his body with obvious approval, then her gaze stops at his crotch. On his boner, to be precise. She swallows and blinks slowly. Finally looking back to me, she smirks. "You weren't kidding about the goods. Have fun with that." She blows me a kiss then leaves, the apartment door slamming shut behind her.

Epilogue

SIMON'S WEDDING

Reagan

Weddings make me nervous. They are the perfect place for embarrassing things to happen. And if it's going to happen, it's going to happen to me.

At least I don't really know anyone here. I met Simon and Jessie last weekend. But other than them, I only know Rhett, and he's on best man duty most of the day.

Jessie was super-lovely, though, and said I could tag along to the photo shoot and even sit with Rhett at the reception. She'd been terrified Rhett was going to bring some whore he'd picked up the night before to the wedding, and since he brought me instead, I get special privileges.

Rhett and I have been a couple for two weeks, and I've never been happier. I can't stop staring at him. He's so damn sexy, and he knows it. His tux is fitted to perfection. The way it moulds around his biceps is giving me all kinds of spank-bank material. Not that I need it; Rhett is just as ravenous in bed as I am.

And oh my God, those pants. I've been resisting the urge to sink my teeth into his arse since he put them on. Watching him walk away wasn't the hardship I was expecting it to be when he left me at my seat ten minutes ago to join the other groomsmen.

He catches my eye from his place beside Simon on the podium, while everyone waits for Jessie to arrive, and blows me a kiss. I pretend to catch it, glance around to make sure nobody is looking, then tug up the hem of my dress and release it up my skirt.

He chokes on a laugh, and Simon elbows him. I smirk, then wink. He just shakes his head and smiles wider.

I'm sitting in the fourth row, all by myself. I don't know if it's because I'm the only visibly tattooed person at this wedding or just because nobody knows me. I don't really mind, though. Saves me making a fool of myself trying to make small talk. I keep my eyes on Rhett when the music starts, signalling Jessie's arrival.

I only look away when she strides down the aisle, and I see her stunning dress. It's beautiful. I've never seen anything like it. When I met Jessie, I thought for sure she would be the kind of woman to wear a super-traditional, white dress. But she looks like Cinder-freaking-ella in a light blue gown that puffs out at her small hips in layer upon layer of tulle encrusted with sparkly gems.

When Rhett finally looks at her, his eyes widen, and he shoves Simon's shoulder. Simon glares at him for a split second before going back to staring at Jessie in wonder. It's so cute, the way he looks at her like she's the light of his life.

Then, my eyes meet Rhett's again, and that's exactly how he's looking at me.

"I love you," he mouths to me, and I swear my heart stops beating in my chest.

Clutching my throat, I blink back tears. *"I love you too,"* I mouth back.

Rhett

I DID IT. I TOLD HER I LOVE HER. I COULDN'T hold it back a second longer when I saw the look in her eyes. She is everything.

As soon as the ceremony's done, and the minister says, *"You may now kiss the bride"*, I bound down the stairs, not caring that I was supposed to stay there for a bunch of photos.

I've got Reagan wrapped in my arms a moment later, my fingers intertwined in her silky locks, probably messing up her hairdo, but fuck it. I press my mouth to hers and take in all her sweetness, releasing a moan I can't contain.

Gliding my tongue over her pouty bottom lip, I suck it and groan when she digs her fingers into my back beneath my suit coat. "I fucking love you," I breathe into her parted lips. "So much, Reagan. So fucking much."

Her smiling is blinding, and I feel it like a punch to the chest.

"I love you too," she murmurs before pushing up on her tiptoes to take my mouth again.

So fucking perfect.

The End

Acknowledgments

Writing is not always easy, even for those of us that can't live without it. It's challenging, frustrating, exhausting, and sometimes—downright painful.

I needed a break from writing Rom/Sus. It's the genre I'm more popular in and write most frequently. I didn't need the break because I'd fallen out of love with it, more like we just needed a Ross and Rachel style break. I fully intend to return to Rom/Sus.

I kind of feel like writing Pink Bits and enjoying the process so much was like Ross cheating on Rachel (He totally cheated, they were on a break, not broken up!).

Anyway, I don't regret it. I refuse. I LOVE this book. So much so that I'm going to give Charlotte a story too. I'm extending our "break" and staying in RomCom for a little bit. That's not to say I won't go back to Rom/Sus, because I most certainly will.

With all of that said I need to thank my two book world sisters—Anastasia Austin and Liz Lovelock. They keep me going. When I'm down, they lift me up or give me the space I need to get through it.

When I'm smashing the words, they're right there, cheering me on with pink pompoms.

I'd be lost without them. They will forever be a part of my writing process and more importantly, part of my life.

And to you, for taking the time to read this book —Thank You.

Xox
 JB

Also by JB HELLER

ROM COMS

AWKWARD GIRLS

Pink Bits

Blue Beaver

Silver Bush

UNEXPECTED LOVERS

The Starfish Method

The Covert Cam Girl

The Unexpected Manny

The Ballbuster's Dilemma

Falling For His Fake Fiancé

Wooing His Accidental Wife

SHILOH SPRINGS WORLD

HUNTERS & CO.

Catastrophe Magnet

Hacker Heart

Red Hot Rebel

Poker Face

STANDALONE

What If It's Right?

BROKEN BOYS / MOMENTS

Broken Boys Break Hearts

Broken Boys Fight Harder

Broken Boys Despise Deceit

Broken Boys Crave Chaos

The Parlor (Standalone coming 2023)

ROMANTIC SUSPENSE

ATTRACTION SERIES

Complete Series

Undeniable Attraction

Pure Attraction

Fierce Attraction

ALPHA ONE PROTECTION

(Attraction Series Spin Off)

Worth The Risk

Worth The Wait

JB Heller is an average Aussie housewife and Momma in her mid 30's with a wicked sexy imagination.

These days she writes mostly contemporary romance and romantic comedies, drawing inspiration from her everyday life.

Monday to Friday you can find JB glued to her laptop weaving words or trolling Pinterest for her next potential muse. Come the weekend, it's family time. (And of course lots of reading and Netflix binges.)

Want to know more?

Monthly Newsletter Sign Up:
https://bit.ly/3FtVhyd
Facebook Reader Group:
Heller's Bookwhorders

Made in the USA
Coppell, TX
29 March 2023